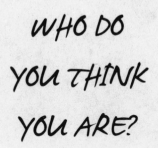

WHO DO
YOU THINK
YOU ARE?

WHO DO YOU THINK YOU ARE?

PAULINE BURGESS

POOLBEG

Published 2018
by Poolbeg Press Ltd
123 Grange Hill, Baldoyle
Dublin 13, Ireland
E-mail: poolbeg@poolbeg.com

© PAULINE BURGESS 2018

The moral right of the author has been asserted.

Typesetting, editing, layout, design, ebook © Poolbeg Press Ltd.

1

A catalogue record for this book is available from the British Library.

ISBN 978-1-78199-811-3

Typeset by Poolbeg

Printed and bound by CPI Group (UK) Ltd, Croydon, CR0 4YY

www.poolbeg.com

About the author

Pauline Burgess is a writer and teacher from County Down who is inspired every single day by the children around her, including her daughter and her students. The Arts Council of Northern Ireland recognised her passion for writing for children when they granted her the Artists' Career Enhancement Award in 2013. Her series for younger readers – *Pony Friends Forever* – has become extremely popular with primary schools all over Northern Ireland, and *Pony Surprise* was an Eason top-ten bestseller. Pauline regularly visits schools and libraries across Ireland in her capacity as an author and active proponent of reading for pleasure.

Her first novel for teenagers, *Knock Back*, was published by Poolbeg in 2017.

Acknowledgements

I would like to thank Paula, Caroline and everyone at Poolbeg Press for their continued support, friendship and scintillating chats – chats that often have nothing to do with books, but everything to do with writing. As always, thank you to Gaye for always helping to gently guide and shape my novels into something infinitely more readable.

Very grateful thanks also go to Dana Williamson, Gabriela McNulty and Paulina Rys for 'Polish-proofing' this book; to Dana for introducing me to *pierogi* and to Gabby for allowing me to borrow her home town of Gizycko and keeping me right on my descriptions of Masuria. To all of you – your support has been invaluable!

As always, thank you to my family who support my writing journeys, particularly to Paul and Emma who feel every bump on the road with me. Particular thanks go to my parents who gave me roots – but allowed me to grow in my own way.

Thanks, as always, to my friends (writerly and otherwise) for your incredible support.

But, most of all, I would like to thank every East European student I have ever taught, because *you* inspired this book. Magda represents each and every one of you, and I hope that her resilience, courage and tenacity go some way towards representing yours. Thank you for bringing your language, your culture and your adaptability to my little corner of the world.

For my mum and dad
– because your roots are my roots

To thine own self be true.
William Shakespeare

Chapter one

Something small and hard spun past me, bouncing off the wall as soon as I stepped out through our front door.

Crouching down, I hauled my hood up and took cover against the redbrick wall of the shop, then sort of peered out from under the hood to see if the coast was clear. No-one.

Skulking along the street I did another quick scan. But whoever had thrown that stone had moved on, forgetting about me and mine for another day. Or maybe just until this afternoon – when I'd return from school and be their target practice all over again. Glancing back at our flat above the shop to make sure Mama and my granddad hadn't seen what happened, I rolled the stone around in my hand and pocketed it with some of the others. Dziadek – that's 'grandfather' in Polish and is pronounced *Jad-dek* – loved precious gemstones. Me, I just got stuck with the 'missile' variety.

Adults scurried past me as I reached the Donegall Road, their chins buried into their collars. One or two girls from my school were heading in the same direction, with their eyes screwed up against the rain. Needless to say, they didn't wait for me. Passing cars tossed spray in my direction as if I wasn't even there. Dziadek was always saying how lucky I was to be living in Ireland now, but he didn't have to face stone-throwing and, worse, being ignored on a daily basis. In fact, he might as well have been back in Poland for all the time he spent outside the flat. Living in his little attic room on the top floor for the past few years, he surrounded himself with memories of home. Half the time he was convinced he *was* home.

I jumped on the hot-pink Belfast city bus and, as per usual, it was standing room only. Stopping and starting at every junction, the bus jerked its way along streets shiny with rain. Bars and KFCs began to give way to expensive boutiques and then leafier roads and the double-fronted Victorian houses where most of my classmates lived. I say class 'mates' but they weren't mates. They were the direct opposite, really. At best they were 'polite' and distant. At worst they were just Belview Bitches.

My school, Belview College for Girls, sat on the opposite side of Chester Road from the Belfast Academy for Boys. The two buildings mouldered in this morning's rain, watching each other across the leafy road as if bracing themselves for a fight. Boys in black blazers turned left when they disembarked from the bus, and girls in green blazers and white shirts turned right to cross to Belview College on the other side.

After dropping my overcoat in the cloakroom, I filed behind the other girls into the narrow, polished corridors. Wood-panelled and claustrophobic, these walls enclosed me for over six hours every day, Monday to Friday. The strange thing was, I actually liked the place. As long as I ignored most of the other girls, kept my head down and soaked up what I was being taught, it was a kind of refuge. Not as safe and happy as being with Dziadek, but good in other ways. I loved the waxy polished smells and the dusty library filled to the brim with tomes as old as the school. And the wall-to-wall encyclopaedias that nobody even used these days because Google had the answer to *everything*. Then there were the long, glassy science labs that smelt of chemicals and tubes and burners. In fact, I'd be heading to the labs straight after registration. Triple Science to start the week. Not everybody's thing, but I actually liked mixing drops of this and drops of that in beakers and seeing what might happen. And Anna, the girl I sat beside in science, wasn't bad. Well, she sort of talked to me at least.

My form room throbbed with huddles of Belview Babes strung around desks or perched on radiators. As usual I went straight to my seat at the window.

Miss Kennedy strode in then, thin as a wire, set her planner down and turned to us with her usual menace. We called her the Wicked Witch of the West behind her back, because she was from the west of the city – not entirely imaginative.

'Morning, 9A.'

Her eyes darted around the room.

'*Morning, 9A!*' she said again, even sharper this time, pursing her lips so that you could see all the cracks in her pink lipstick.

'*Good morning, Miss Kennedy!*' we chanted back.

'Thank you for your laboured reply,' she snarled, then gestured towards a shiny girl who had just walked in to stand beside her. 'This is Sophie,' she went on. 'She's just moved to the area and will be joining this form group. We're already a few weeks into our first term so it will be harder for Sophie to adjust – so I expect you to look out for her and ensure that she receives the hospitality we are renowned for at Belview College.'

Hospitality in Belview College? Seriously? Miss Kennedy waved the new girl in my direction because the seat beside me was empty as always. Go figure.

'Hi,' said the new girl, all dazzling teeth and glossy hair.

'Hi,' I muttered back.

'Magda, will you allow Sophie to copy your timetable into her school planner, please?' Miss Kennedy asked. 'And keep an eye on her for today.' She then turned away, leaving me to be the beginner's buddy for the day.

'Magda – is that a foreign name?' Glossy Girl asked, flicking her shiny hair,

'Polish,' I answered, rolling my eyes. It didn't take anyone long to pick up on my *otherness*. 'I prefer to be called Maggie,' I mumbled.

'Why?'

Duuh, I thought. Because it sounds more *local*? I just glared at her instead, letting her know that I didn't expect or want her to ask me questions all day.

Miss Kennedy went through the usual registration routine before the bell, reminding us for the umpteenth time about standards.

'Come on,' I said to Sophie as soon as the bell stopped ringing. 'Science.'

I shuffled away from the table, silently wondering how long it would take her to make real friends and learn to ignore me like the rest of the class. She walked beside me, asking polite questions about teachers and classes and beaming away with her sparkling smile. Her red-brown hair was so shiny it reminded me of the chestnuts back on the trees along our street in Gizycko. Conkers, they called them here – not that I saw too many on our South Belfast street. Flattened beer cans were more likely.

'Gosh, I hope it's not too much like my old school,' Sophie was blathering on. 'It was *sooo* strict. Are they nice here?' She flicked her hair again. 'The teachers, I mean?'

'They're just ... teachers,' I shrugged, baffled as to what difference it made what they were *like*. I mean, who really cared? They were just there to teach you stuff and then turn to the next class and do it all over again. Programmed. Indifferent.

'Gosh, it's such an old building, isn't it?' she gasped, looking around her. 'There must be millions of stories in these walls!'

Was she *actually* for real? Who the heck said 'gosh' outside of an Enid Blyton novel? She must have caught my withering look because she started apologising for asking too many questions.

'God, Magda, I'm so sorry. My mum says I talk way too much. Especially when I'm nervous.'

She did that thing with her hair again, like a shampoo ad, and flashed me her brilliant white teeth.

'Tell me more about *yo*u, Magda,' she said, her grey-blue eyes dancing.

'There's nothing to tell. And I'm Maggie, not Magda.'

'Oh, sorry, Maggie. And what's your surname, Maggie? Mine's Long – yeah, I know, so geeky, isn't it? Sophie *Loooonnng*. I hate it.'

'Jankowska,' I answered. She was beginning to feel like a prickly rash.

We reached the Science lab and I made my escape, sitting down on the bench at the back beside Anna. I figured Mr Scott would allocate Little Miss Sunshine a seat and I'd be free of her blather until breaktime at least. But he pulled a spare stool over and squashed her in beside Anna and me.

'Hi, I'm Sophie Long!' Sophie sang out, reaching a hand over to Anna.

Anna kind of glanced up from under her thick brown fringe, just long enough to give a barely perceptible nod of the head.

'Are you and Maggie friends?' Sophie asked. 'I hope you don't mind me squeezing in beside you?'

Anna looked as confounded as me. We weren't used to Glossy Girls apologising for sitting beside us.

'It's OK,' Anna said, glancing sideways at me with something like shock in her eyes.

Anna was as mousey as Sophie was glamorous, and me, well, I was the foreign one. I still got one or two slang words mixed up and I'd never really got the hang of 'banter' – I never knew whether people were being mean to each other or just having a laugh. Apparently calling each other a *melt* or a *dose* was one-part affection, three parts offence.

Mr Scott took the register and clicked an image onto the interactive whiteboard.

'The human digestive system,' he announced, pointing his pen at the screen.

A cartoon naked man appeared with his stomach, pancreas and intestines on show. And other bits down below which sent the Belview Blondes in the front row into hysterics. Surprisingly Sophie tutted and mumbled something about immaturity, making me think I had misjudged her.

'Food is digested in the mouth, stomach and small intestine,' Mr Scott went on, ignoring the front row. 'Digested food is absorbed into the bloodstream in the small intestine and excess water is absorbed back into the body in the large intestine.' Pausing for effect, he added, 'Any undigested food passes out of the anus when we go to the toilet.'

More tittering followed. Mr Scott rolled his eyes before telling us to copy the diagram down.

'Sir?' Mia Campbell asked, all pretend innocence. 'Do we have to draw the man's wee *thing* as well?'

'Just concentrate on the organs of the digestive system which are clearly marked in red, Mia. And, for goodness' sake, a little maturity might be appropriate.'

'Are they always like that?' Sophie whispered in my ear.

'Like what?'

'Like *sooo* annoying. Don't they realise how dorky they sound?'

'Erm, yeah. They do. And yes, they are. Always like that, I mean.'

'Dunno how you listen to them,' she said. She had drawn a perfect outline of a man with his insides on show. She tightened her lips in concentration as she drew coiled intestines inside a larger ring of sausage rolls leading down towards a rectum.

'You're really good,' I said.

'At drawing? Yeah, I love it,' she answered. 'But not half as good as Nicola. She's an artist.'

'Is that your sister?'

'No, my mum.'

She called her mother by her first name?

'There's just Nicola and me at home,' she went on. 'Ben – my dad – is in Thailand.'

'Cool,' I blurted, not really knowing what else to say.

'So what are *you* good at?' she asked me, still sketching.

'I … I don't know really.' I shrugged my shoulders and thought about the fact that no-one had ever really asked me that question before.

'Well, it's my mission to find out,' she smiled, her grey-blue eyes glinting at me. 'So where do we go at breaktime?'

We? She still wanted to hang around me at breaktime?

'The Tuck …' I answered, not really sure what to add.

'Then maybe just hang around the netball courts?' Anna suggested, her voice cautious, clearly frightened of being too pushy. 'It's stopped raining.'

'Sounds good!' Sophie nodded, erasing and redrawing the man's thighs like she was doing a piece for GCSE Art.

I glanced at Anna, my eyebrows raised like question marks. This was not an everyday experience for us – the glossiest girl in the class asking *us* for advice and company. We knew it wouldn't last long, but I figured she might as well follow us around for a bit. Even Anna and I normally parted company at the end of Science lessons. It had never really occurred to us to hang about together. Maybe it should have.

Three periods of science later and heads full to bursting with proteins and enzymes, we left the lab as a group of three and headed along the covered walkway in the direction of the Tuck, Anna and I flanking Sophie Long and being stared at by all the in-girls.

Sophie bought a packet of Tayto Cheese and Onion and followed us over to the netball courts. It was still warm enough to sit on the ground and idle away the next fifteen minutes before French class. Anna sat peeling her giant orange in silence and I sipped on my smoothie. All the while Sophie chirped away about all sorts of drivel. When I looked up into the weak September sun to see Mia and her Miseries watching us from the far corner of the netball courts, I could almost feel my lips curling into a smile.

Chapter two

'*Magda? Czy to ty?*' Is that you?

'Yes, Mama,' I called back, as I went into our flat above the shop.

Mama worked in the shop part-time, which suited her down to the ground because it was a Polish shop so her English was never stretched too much. Her friend Michal ran the shop. He was a friend of a friend from back home in Poland and he had the flat and the job all sorted for us even before we arrived in Belfast. When Mama wasn't working, she was cooking, and right now the smell of *kartoflanka* – potato soup – was wafting its way from our tiny kitchen area at the back of the flat and right into my nostrils. She said Dziadek needed a good,

13

strong broth to build him up again. He had become really skinny in the last few months and my mother seriously believed that potatoes were the answer to everything. I'm convinced it was one of the reasons we ended up in Ireland.

'Good day?' she asked.

I nodded my head and realised that actually it *had* been a good day. Plus, no stones on my way home, so one of my better days in fact. I looked around at the compact room with the seventies-looking cream fireplace in the centre and sighed with relief that I was safe in here, away from the morons who didn't like *foreners* – their spelling, not mine.

I threw my schoolbag on the sofa and tore up the stairs to the attic to see Dziadek.

As usual he was sitting bleary-eyed, looking at old photos of home. I bent to kiss his forehead and breathed in the familiar smell of him: a mix of pipe tobacco and aftershave.

'Hello, my love,' he said in Polish, putting his arm around my shoulders. 'Doesn't she look just like you?'

He was looking at my grandma, also called Magda, when she was about seventeen or eighteen. They were already married by then, but it was before their children came along. She had the same light-brown hair and high cheekbones as me and

14

Mama, but I always thought she looked tougher. More resilient. I guess she'd had to be. She lost her own parents before she'd even turned sixteen and then had to fight her extended family over the right to marry a much older man – Dziadek. Mama always said that she was a no-nonsense sort of person and that Dziadek literally adored the ground she walked on.

'Have you been sitting here all day, Dziadek?' I asked, pushing some of his thick white hair back from his face. He was in his usual seat by the window – wing-backed, in rich plum fabric that was full of moth-holes.

'Where else is there to go, Magda?' he said, shrugging his shoulders. 'It's all noise and rushing around out there. It makes my head spin.'

He was right. There were no parks where we lived, no quiet roads to walk along. But I still hated the thought of him locking himself into this attic room all day. He said he preferred to look at old photographs instead of the city's sprawl below. Or he would stare happily for hours at the huge map of Poland on the wall behind his bed. Better than staring at red tiles and crooked gables apparently.

'I wish we had a car,' I moaned, curling up in the other smaller chair he kept by the window for me. 'Then we could go to nice places, the seaside even.

Bangor or Newcastle, maybe. Just *somewhere* away from here!'

'You go to a nice place every day, Magda,' he said, looking up at me with his rheumy eyes. 'You're a lucky, lucky girl to go to a school like that.'

He was right and I knew that, really ... but where we lived – I just hated it. I had never let go of the resentment I felt about leaving our lovely little town in Masuria in the north of Poland. And, yet, I was desperately trying to forget my Polishness now that I was here in Belfast.

'A muddle of misery,' Dziadek called me in the days when we first arrived here. 'It's good to embrace new things,' he'd said, 'but it's good to remember where we came from too.'

Dziadek hadn't embraced Belfast at all, but I didn't bother pointing that out. He didn't need me to.

'Toni says he's saving hard for a second-hand car,' I said. 'He's been scanning the papers looking for a bargain. Problem is, Tata isn't so keen ...' I tailed off.

Tata – that means 'Dad' – had this thing about us not *getting above our station* here in Belfast. He acted like we were second-class citizens and even the thought of owning a car brought him out in a rash. I hated the way he thought we should know our place and be meek and mild.

'It's early days yet for your brother at work,' Dziadek said. 'Too soon for him to think about buying something costing as much as a car.'

I rolled my eyes at my family's obvious inferiority complex. Just because we were Polish didn't mean we had to be second-rate. Tata and Toni worked every hour they could, mowing lawns and clipping hedges for the richer folks in the suburbs. Tata had been a teacher back in Masuria, but here he worked with soil from dawn to dust. It wasn't like we were bloody scroungers. Yet I always felt like that.

I got up and knelt by his chair. 'What about taking the bus, Dziadek? I know you're a bit nervous about taking public transport, but I'll be with you to translate. We could take ourselves right out into the countryside?'

'*No!*' he said sharply. 'I have told you, Magda. *No!*'

Since my grandmother died, back home in Masuria, he seemed to have lost his nerve and I couldn't bear to see him wasting away. The only thing that brought a sparkle to his eyes was when we talked about her. And about Poland.

'Look, Magda. I'm sorry. But it is too late for me to start again here,' he mumbled, shaking his head. 'You, though, you must grab your chances, my

17

love.' He ruffled my hair like I was still a toddler. 'You must make life here,' he went on, now speaking in English. 'Don't worry about this old man. Go out and grab this country with every skin in your body.'

I knew he meant *bone* in your body, but there was no need to point it out. Dziadek was telling me that he had given up. But that there was still a chance for me. His eyes were wet with memories and I wished with all my heart that we hadn't dragged him away from everything he knew. Wearing two old cardigans to keep himself warm, he looked cold and lost sitting in this room, surrounded by threadbare carpet and mismatching furniture.

I thought of the 'better life' Tata had said we'd have in Ireland. It wasn't much of a life for Dziadek.

When Mama called us for our *kartoflanka*, I took him by the hand and tugged him a little, then led him slowly down the narrow stairs.

'I have to work late in the shop tomorrow, Magda,' Mama said, ladling out the thick, steamy broth. She sat two bowls down on the drop-leaf table for us and a plate of home-made bread which she placed in the centre. 'Your father and Toni will be working late too, so will you make sure Dziadek eats?'

'Yes, Mama!' I sang, rolling my eyes. As if I would let him starve! At least two nights every week I was on granddad duty and she gave me the same instruction *every* time! 'Where are they anyway?' I was wondering why it was only the three of us this evening for 'tea', as they called it in Belfast.

'Finishing Mr Ferguson's garden.' She smiled as she said this.

One thing my mother valued above all else – even potatoes – was hard work. She was so proud that my dad and Toni had found good jobs within weeks of coming to Belfast. She kept talking about the day when I would leave school too and get myself a *good* job. The only problem was, she saw this happening when I was sixteen whereas I wanted to get my GCSEs and A Levels and go to college. Even if it meant being stuck with the Belview Blondes for almost another five years. Mama, on the other hand, left school at fifteen to work for her parents. As the youngest of ten children, it was expected that she should stay close to home and become their nursemaid in their old age. Well, she got the second part right, but she wasn't exactly close to home. Home was Gizycko in the heart of the Masurian Lakes, not the back streets of Belfast.

'*Katarina!*' My father's voice boomed up the stairs, his feet bounding up them just as loudly.

19

'They're back early,' Mama said. 'I thought they said they'd be working late.'

'*Katarina, Magda, come see!*' my father yelled, bursting in through the door with a grin as wide as the Lagan footbridge. 'Come, both of you!' He led Dziadek over to the window. 'You look out here, OK?'

I flew past him and down the stairs, through the front door and onto the street.

Toni was slouched against a rusty, green Toyota car, looking like the cat that got the cream.

'What's going on?' Though I could guess.

'*This* is going on, Magda,' my brother answered in English, spreading his hand on the bonnet of the car and rubbing it like it was priceless. 'This is the new family wagon.' Then he added in a stupid voice: 'We are now *mobile*.'

'Are you sure?' I laughed. 'I don't think that thing would get us any farther than the City Hall.'

'Hey, this cost a bomb, *dziewczynka* – don't mock it!'

Dziewczynka means 'little girl'. It should have annoyed me when he called me that, but strangely, it didn't.

'Don't worry, Katarina,' Tata was saying. 'We can afford it. And it will be good to get your grandfather out of the flat from time to time.' He was rubbing

20

Mama's arm, sensing the panic she was feeling about the expense. He had obviously changed his mind about *getting above our station.*

'You are right,' Mama nodded, her eyes tearing up. 'This is what we need for Papa.' She glanced upwards to the small window where her father looked down on us like a ghost. There was an expression of vague curiosity on his face as he stood there peering at us. She turned again to Tata and asked fearfully, 'But, how can you guarantee that you will keep getting jobs, Tomasz?'

Tata grinned, shaking his head at her. 'Always worry, worry, worry, Katarina.' He laughed, his brown eyes dancing with excitement. 'Today Toni and I got a job for life!'

Mama's hands flew up to her face. 'What? Where? How?' she cried, hardly breathing.

'At Belview College!' he cried. 'I will be gardener and Toni caretaker for the school! What do you think of that, little Magda?'

He turned to me for approval. He didn't get it.

'No way!' I cried, backing away. *'No way! Not Belview College!'*

What the heck was he thinking of? This would be humiliation on a mega scale!

'What is wrong, Magda?' Mama asked.

'What is wrong?' I screeched. *'It's bad enough ...'* I

21

couldn't even find the words. 'The girls leave me alone most of the time – but now – Belview College? Oh my God, this can't be happening! The gardener's daughter? *They can't work there, they just can't!*'

Tata and Toni stared at me like I'd lost the plot, poor Tata's face slipping from pride into concern.

'*I'll be a laughing stock!*' I shouted. 'Don't you get it? Their dads are accountants and consultants and … and I don't know what else! Not bloody gardeners!' I turned and ran inside.

'*Magda, come back here!*' Mama was shouting, her face white with shock. 'Don't you dare be so rude to your father!'

I didn't care. I ran up the stairs, swishing my ponytail like a weapon and swearing I would never forgive them.

Tata and Toni wandering around Belview College? Over my dead body!

Chapter three

'Hi, Maggie!'

Glossy Girl sauntered towards me like something out of a slo-mo fashion shoot, her glinting hair tumbling around her shoulders.

'Hi,' I muttered back, barely glancing sideways.

'All ready for double Art? I just love Miss Price! She's so enthusiastic about everything, isn't she?'

I just sighed. I wasn't up for this amount of sparkle first thing in the morning. Especially after the revelation from Tata and Toni the week before. They were due to start at Belview within the next few days.

'Yeah,' was about all I could muster.

'I bet you're really creative, Maggie – being foreign and all,' she babbled.

'*Foreign*? You say that like it's an exotic disease or something. Are you actually taking the piss?' I hated the way some people tried to be 'nice' to *foreigners* when really they thought we were a sub-species or something.

'God, no, Maggie. I'm … I'm sorry, I didn't mean to …'

'Well, you did,' I answered. 'You *did* insult me, like practically everyone else in this stupid city! I'm not *foreign* – I'm just me!'

I marched off just as her eyes started to fill up. In a way I was glad of the excuse to fall out with her – it was bound to happen sooner or later anyway. She'd been traipsing around after me for a week but she'd soon tire of a no-mark like me. Better to send her on her glorious way to the Belview Bounces with their Pantene hair. I dragged myself down the Year 9 corridor towards my form room, jostling past the It girls with their shiny eyebrows and the swaggering jockettes carrying their kitbags. The classroom smelt of beeswax and deodorant with its usual mix of posh chirping Chester Roadies, and out-of-towners who actually *paid* for the privilege to board at Belview. I threw my bag down on the desk and sat down in my seat by the window. Two ancient oak trees towered above, creating dappled shadows on the lawn outside. In a few weeks' time the leaves would be gone and the trees on Chester Road would revert to spare, spindly boughs. By then, Dziadek would be coughing again and turning ever more inwards.

I heard a chair creak beside me.

'Maggie, I'm really sorry. I – I really didn't mean to be offensive. I just let my motor-mouth run away with me sometimes.'

Sophie was staring right into me in a way that made me blush. Her forehead had creased into a hundred frown lines.

'Please. You're my only friend here,' she pleaded. 'Give me another chance?'

Jeez, she was nothing if not persistent. And where did she learn to beg like that?

'It's alright,' I shrugged. 'Forget it.'

I pulled my planner out of my bag for a last-minute check on today's homework and hoped she'd just sit back and chill. She was way too emotional for me – all happy-clappy one minute and waterfalls the next.

'The French homework was hard, wasn't it?' she asked, a bit calmer now.

'Yeah,' I grunted, although really it wasn't.

Class work, home work – they were never really that challenging for me. I didn't know how or why but learning just seemed to come easy to me. Not that I made a song and dance out of it – that would just be another excuse for my classmates to have a go at me. Never mind hiding your light under a bushel, I hid mine deep down in the earth as far as the roots would penetrate. When I'd passed the Transfer Test and was given a place at Belview, I came out in hives with embarrassment. My old Primary 7 teacher was as shocked as I was, having told my mum not to enter me for the test because my English still wasn't up to scratch. I had only joined the school in Primary 5 and I guess I was just written off because I was so quiet and they assumed I couldn't understand a word they were saying. I could. I just didn't show it.

'Why is Anna not in our Art class?' Sophie was asking, folding down a page in her planner.

'Just isn't. She's in 9B so she's just with us for Science and Home Economics,' I answered.

'Oh, good. I have you all to myself then,' she said, beaming.

Seriously!

We scraped our chairs back and gathered our things after the 9.10 bell and headed for the stairs to Block D where the Art and Science rooms were. The usual chit-chat about the Kardashians and Youtubers was going on as we climbed up the right-hand side of the staircase. Left side was for coming down. Belview College had it all sorted.

'Do you want to come over to mine at the weekend?' Sophie asked out of the blue.

'Erm …'

'Oh, please don't say no. We'll have *soo* much fun!' She looked right into me again, like she could see beneath my skin.

'I don't know where you live,' I said, shrugging pathetically.

'That's no bother – I'll PM you my address – it's not far from here anyway,' she gushed, crooking her arm into mine. 'How about lunchtime Saturday? I make great Sweet Chilli Wraps. We can take them out the garden if it's dry and just – hang out.'

Why did she always have to sound so bloody American?

'OK,' I found myself answering. 'But just write your address down in my homework diary,' I added, not bothering to mention that I didn't own a mobile phone. 'I suppose Antoni, my brother, could drop me off on Saturday.'

But the thought of Toni's battered, green Toyota coughing up Sophie's driveway was enough to make me rethink. Not that I knew for certain that she had a driveway, but if she lived around this area then it was probably tree-lined and sweet-smelling, leading to a great, big redbrick with ivy artistically crawling up the walls.

Miss Price was knee-deep in our Homes and Houses project when we walked in. Our desks were covered in cut-out pieces of photographs which we were told to reassemble.

'Think about the features of the houses to help you reassemble them,' she was saying. 'Where will the door go? The chimney etc. I know it seems like a very simple exercise, girls, but I want to get you thinking about the lines, the patterns, the shape and form.'

Up here in the Art room the sun was able to flood in, unhindered by trees. This section of the building was more modern than the rest, built sometime in the seventies. It was lighter and brighter, or maybe Miss Price just made it feel that way. Her curly red hair was loosely tied back with long wisps escaping round her face.

'We're going to be studying all kinds of homes, as I told you last week – everything from igloos to tepees to modern bungalows!' she called out in a sing-song voice. 'Then at the end of the unit of work you'll create your own ideal home, from whichever materials you choose here in this room.'

She spread her arms wide to indicate our choices and smiled her gap-toothed grin, like she'd just had the best idea in the world. Sophie was *actually* clasping her hands together in delight and grinning at Miss Price like she was a goddess.

'I'm going to try to make a copy of our house,' she whispered. 'With all its Victorian features and everything.'

'Yeah, I think I'll do our dingy flat, with all its rising damp,' I replied.

Again she gave me that wounded look and I actually began to feel a bit mean. I decided that maybe I should give Sophie a break.

We worked in pairs putting the photograph of a large, white house back together and talking about what should go where. When we had the whole thing done she high-fived me like some pre-teen.

'You don't like me very much, do you, Maggie?' Her smile had thinned.

'I … no, I, yes … I do.'

'No, you don't. Miss Kennedy made you look after me, so you feel you're stuck with me.' She was shaking her head as she began to fill out the report sheet on the task we'd just completed. 'It's OK. I don't mind.'

'No,' I protested. 'It's just that, well, it's me. I'm not very good at making friends. I'm not used to actually *having* friends.'

'Did you have friends in Poland?'

'Of course I did!'

'Then why not here?' she asked.

'*Duuh*. Isn't it obvious? Do you think these

29

Belvies would want to be friends with a *Pole*?'

She turned fully towards me now. 'Maybe they would, Maggie, but you're so busy being angry with all of them that you don't give them a chance.'

'God, you're such an idealist, Sophie,' I answered, rolling my eyes. 'You've got it all wrong. They expect me to keep quiet and out of their way, and that's what I do.'

'Yes, you keep out of their way, but how do you know that's what they really want? And what about me? You know I'm new here and you just shrug me off all the time.'

'But you could be friends with *them*,' I said, touchily.

'But I want to be friends with *you*!'

I was exasperated now. 'Why?'

'Why not? You're kind, even though you're trying really hard not to be. You're clever, you're funny and you're interesting.'

The big white grin was back. Maybe this girl *was* for real. Maybe she actually was Little Miss Sunshine and not just an act.

'So, what type of house are you going to make at the end of the project?' she asked, like we hadn't just embarrassed each other.

'I dunno,' I said. 'Maybe my granddad will have some ideas.'

'Cool. Is he old?' she asked, pulling all her hair to one side and twisting it into a long roll.

'Yeah, he is actually. My mum's his youngest child so he's older than you'd expect. He turned eighty in the summer.'

'Does he live here? In Ireland?'

'Yeah, he lives with us.'

'That's brave,' she said, raising her eyebrows. 'To move to another country when you're, like, *ancient*!'

'Yeah,' I answered. 'Yeah, it is.'

But I couldn't help thinking about Dziadek's glassy eyes. Staring into nothing. Maybe he had been brave – but had *we* been stupid, dragging him all the way here? Away from his language, his culture? Tata had said at the time that some of Mama's siblings would surely take him in, but she wouldn't hear of it. She said that, as the youngest, it was her responsibility to look after him. Tata didn't get the logic and neither did I, but I knew one thing: if Dziadek hadn't come with us, I wouldn't have come either. Maybe *that* was what was behind Mama's thinking.

Miss Price handed out more photos – intact this time – of different types of homes around the world, from tents to tower blocks.

'Now, pick one that really appeals to you,' she lilted. 'One that just jumps out at you. You don't even need to explain why.' She smiled. 'And then draw it!'

She laughed as she issued the challenge, reassuring us that it didn't matter how accurate the drawing was, as long as it was our own interpretation.

Sophie picked a palace – no surprise there – while I went for a wooden treehouse sheltering in a forest. I started sketching a peaked roof with a box-like structure underneath, while Sophie started on her Disney creation. We were worlds apart in so many ways. And yet when she asked again if I would come round to hers on Saturday, I said yes. Even though the very thought of it made my heart race just that little bit faster.

Chapter four

'Seriously, Toni, didn't you check this thing over before you bought it?'

Black smoke was belching out of the back of the Toyota as we darted in and out of city-centre traffic. Toni used the palm of his left hand to turn the steering wheel while the other rested on the roof outside. All he needed was a flippin' medallion round his neck to complete the bozo look. His head rocked backwards and forwards to some lame country music and I wondered how the heck we could even be related.

'Put the bloody window up, Toni. It's freezing!'

'So where to now?' he asked, rolling the window back up.

We were coming up to the junction of the Lisburn Road and University Road.

'That way.' I pointed straight ahead.

We cruised past Queen's University on our left with its gothic red-bricked façade and lawns like billiard tables. We had been taken on a tour there by our form teacher and I knew that I wanted to go there one day. I wanted to stroll around those grounds with a file under my arms and a look of studious nonchalance on my face. I wanted to sip a mochaccino in the student union café, reading something trendy and intellectual. Or sit in the top floor of the university library, looking out over the city and knowing that someday I could leave it. I didn't hate Belfast – I knew it could provide me with all kinds of opportunities for the future, but it wasn't home and never would be. Mind you, neither was Poland any more.

'What number is it?' Toni asked, slowing to a crawl along Chester Road.

'Number 185,' I said, checking the address Sophie had written down for me. 'You can drop me at the gate.'

'No, Magda. I'm not stopping on a main road. I'm pulling in whether you like it or not.'

He knew I was ashamed of the car. And him.

The constant thought of him and Tata coming to work at my school was still gnawing away at me.

But, after that first explosion, I'd managed to keep quiet about my feelings – to the extent that Tata and Toni now thought I was fine with the idea.

Toni swerved into a sweeping pebbled driveway that curved round towards a large redbrick house with double bay windows. The lawn stretched the whole length of the driveway and was so smooth it looked like it had been ironed.

The shiny, black front door flew open and Sophie appeared, waving frantically.

Oh God. Please don't come right out, I was thinking as I jumped out hastily. But she did. Right over to the parked car, beaming in through the window at Toni, who was winding it down and grinning back. (Yes, this rust-bucket actually had wind-down windows.)

'Hi, I'm Sophie!' she announced like a movie star. 'You must be Antoni?'

'Toni,' my brother gushed, a red stain creeping up his neck towards his face.

'You want to come in for a mo?' she asked, all heart-melting smile.

'No! He doesn't!' I stated. Loud and clear.

Toni caught my look and for once he got the message.

'Er … got work to do. I'm sorry,' he stammered, sounding like an imbecile.

'Hang on, Toni – snap happy!' she laughed, taking a photo of him with her phone.

What the heck was that about?

Toni looked as confused as I did, but then he gave Sophie this inane grin and I felt my insides churning. Just to make things worse, he then swerved the car round in a skid, sending pebbles flying everywhere and screeching off like a pathetic boy racer.

'He's cute!'

'He *soo* isn't!'

'Sure he is. You just can't see it, Maggie, because he's your brother.'

She was right – I didn't see it. When I looked at Toni I saw Tata's side of the family, all short and muscular with tight-packed shoulders and a face to match. He was no Zac Efron.

'What does he do?' Sophie asked, taking me by the hand and giggling like a six-year-old.

'He's a gardener. And handy man. Sort of,' I grunted back.

'Oh, that is *sooo* perfect!' She threw her head back and laughed. 'Does he take his shirt off a lot?'

'*Eeuwww!*' This was just way too much. 'Can we stop talking about my dorky brother, please?'

She laughed that high laugh again and led me – yes, *led* me by the hand – into a black-and-white tiled hallway that ran right to the other end of the house. We went straight through and out a glass door to a patio area with outdoor furniture that looked way better than our indoor furniture. There was a rattan sofa and two chairs with cream cushions that must have cost a small fortune and a glass table with a jug of something cool and three light-green frosted glasses on it.

'Nicola made lemonade,' Sophie said, pouring it out and handing me a glass clinking with ice cubes. 'I know it's not summer, but it's such a good day that we thought we could pretend.'

Her mum *made* lemonade? Seriously?

'She'll join us in a minute. She's just on the phone. Go on – sit down,' she beamed.

I sat on one of the chairs. 'What do you do with all this stuff when it rains?' I asked, looking round me at sun loungers and poufs.

'Cover them up, obviously,' she shrugged. 'Well, Charlie does.'

'Who's Charlie?'

'The gardener-cum-caretaker-cum-handyman. But he's positively ancient, and he looks *nothing* like your Toni.'

She threw her feet up on the L-shaped sofa opposite me and looked like she had been born to all this. The back garden was sheltered by pine trees so it was completely private. It was just another world. Two large patio heaters kept the September chill away.

'You like it?' she asked, nodding at the lemonade.

It was bitter-sweet and ice-cold, making me scrunch up my eyes with the first few sips.

'Yeah, refreshing,' I said. 'I've never had homemade lemonade before.'

'You haven't lived, then,' she laughed.

Maybe I hadn't. Being squeezed into a flat that would fit four times into her house probably wasn't living, at least not in the way she meant it.

'What do you wanna talk about?' she asked, throwing herself forward now with gusto.

'Dunno.'

'Boys?'

'I don't really know any.'

'Yeah, that's the worst thing about going to an all-girls school,' she said, rolling her eyes. 'It sucks. There were boys in my last school. One of them – Paul – was really into me. But he hasn't answered any of my messages since I moved school.'

'Why *did* you move school?'

'Erm, just some differences of opinion. Plus, Ben – my dad – thought it wasn't good enough for me.'

She said this like it was the most natural thing in the world. Did that kind of confidence grow with you in a house like this?

'Why did your dad think that?' I asked, wondering why I hadn't heard much about him yet.

'Because I'm his princess and he has high hopes for me,' she said, with another shrug.

'So, why is he in Thailand? Is he on holiday?' I asked, sipping on my lemonade.

'No – *duh* – he lives there,' she smiled.

'Why?' Jeez, I was being dead nosy today – normally I didn't bother asking personal questions.

'He runs a hotel there. Nicola and I used to live with him, but she missed Ireland. We moved back here when I was five.'

This was new. So we *did* have something in common then. We had both moved here from somewhere else. But I would bet all I had that Sophie didn't get stones thrown at her when she left the house.

'Do you miss it?' I asked, trying to forget about the undesirables round our way.

'Sort of. It's gorgeous out there, Maggie. I go out every summer. White sand, gorgeous green seas, guys to die for!' She chuckled. 'Nicola sends me out to Ben for a month at a time. It is absolute heaven!'

'Hello there!' A bright voice echoed behind me. 'You must be Maggie, I'm Nicola!' A small, slim woman with a slick bob bent to air-kiss me. 'Good, you got some lemonade. You guys need anything else?'

'Erm no, thanks,' I muttered like an embarrassed teenager. Which I was, obviously.

'Good, I'll be with you in a sec. Just sorting out an exhibition that's suddenly gone wrong,' she said, pulling a face. 'Why do people let you down at the last minute?' she added, rolling her eyes.

And she disappeared again, bare-footed. If Mama was here she'd be telling the poor woman she was in danger of getting chilblains.

'Nicola's *always* busy!' Sophie said, with a roll of her eyes.

'Why do you call her Nicola?'

'Because it's her name,' she said simply. 'We're just that kind of family. Anyway, let's start prepping for the Sweet Chilli Wraps.'

She jumped up and, grabbing me by the hand, pulled me to my feet and led me into a kitchen the size of a small Tesco, all slate-grey kitchen units and stainless steel. So much for Victorian features.

'*This* is modern,' I said, looking around at brilliant-white walls and floors.

'Yeah, Nicola had it done up a couple of years ago when a lot of her paintings sold well.'

'What kind of paintings does she do?'

'Modern – abstract,' she said, as if they couldn't be anything else. 'She likes the exterior of the house to be Victorian, and the inside to be contemporary, but she hasn't quite got round to transforming it all yet.'

She was pulling down jars and spices and chopping boards from cupboards that seemed to mysteriously fold away and disappear.

'So, was she talking about one of her own exhibitions?' I asked, trying to find a magic utensil drawer.

'Gosh, no. She co-runs a gallery in Bedford Street. It barely leaves her time to work on her own pieces. What does your mum do?'

'She works in a shop,' I answered, feeling strangely apologetic. My mum didn't do *pieces*. Unless you called her soups works of art – which, in a way, they were.

'Here, you get the tortillas out of the pack and heat them. I'll get the turmeric and ginger.'

Now this was out of my comfort zone. *Barszcz* – beetroot soup – was as exotic as we got in our house. And that was only at Christmastime.

'You can heat them in the microwave,' she said, 'but wait until I've done the vegetables.'

I felt myself blush furiously as I said, 'Eh … I don't know how … we don't have a microwave at home.'

Sophie rolled her eyes, but not in an unkind way. 'I'll do it,' she said with a mock sigh.

She chopped onions and yellow peppers and

mixed them in with the spices before throwing them on the pan like an expert.

'Wow! You're good at this,' I said.

She shrugged. 'Like I said, Nicola's always busy so I cook a lot. She did teach me how to make these though.' Her smile was less shiny now. 'So, are you going to make me something delicious when I come to your house? Next weekend maybe?'

'Erm, I'm not much of a cook,' I said pathetically, wondering how on earth I was going to avoid this one. Sparkly Sophie ducking the flying missiles on Radlan Street? Somehow I couldn't see it. 'Maybe we could just meet somewhere instead? Botanic Gardens?'

'Great idea!' she said, flicking her hair as she stirred the vegetables in the pan. 'I love going there. Why don't we take notepads and do some sketching?'

'I'm not that into Art,' I answered, thinking I must sound like a right glum. 'But I'll take my diary and jot some things down.'

'*Ooh*, are you an aspiring writer, Miss Maggie?' she teased, as she began to heat the tortillas.

'Yeah,' I said. 'Yeah, I think I am.'

Now I had never said *that* out loud before. Maybe this friendship with Shiny Sophie wasn't such a bad thing. Maybe it was time to let some of her optimism rub off on me.

'So, have you written anything?' she asked.

'Just one or two stories,' I mumbled. In fact, I'd written over twenty but I was saved from saying anything more about them when Nicola appeared.

'I'm all yours!' she laughed, fetching some more lemonade from the fridge.

After Sophie had ladled the cooked vegetables onto the tortillas, she curled them onto a side of each plate and garnished them with a prepared salad she took from the fridge.

Then we all sat and took a plate each.

'Now, girlies,' Nicola beamed, 'what's the goss?' She looked from Sophie to me all expectantly, her chic brown bob tossing with each turn of the head.

Neither of us answered. I had no idea what to say.

This didn't seem to bother Nicola.

'These look good, Sophie … yum!' she said after she took a bite of tortilla. 'Great as usual.'

I noticed the patch of skin between Sophie's eyebrows had tightened. Then just as quickly the wide smile was back.

'We're planning our day out next weekend, Nicola. Wanna come?'

'Where are you going, honey?'

'Botanic Gardens.'

'I wouldn't miss it!' Nicola declared.

I was sure I heard Sophie mutter something

under her breath, but her mum didn't seem to notice. Or maybe I had just imagined it. Then Sophie locked her grey-blue eyes on to her mum's and I felt sure there was something I was missing.

Chapter five

Toni parked his car three streets away to keep it 'safe'. Mama didn't understand, but then Mama didn't know about the stone-throwing or name-calling. Or any of it really. Toni told her there was just more space for parking nearer the Lisburn Road.

'I'll bring it round and park it in front of the shop, Ma,' he said now, 'so Dziadek won't have far to walk.'

'Newcastle's over thirty miles away, Toni. Will that banger of yours get us there and back?' I joked.

'If you don't trust it, then don't come,' he said over his shoulder with a shrug.

To be fair, he'd given it a good check-up and clean inside and out, and it no longer belched smoke.

He bounced down the street, full of importance.

Our Toni wasn't the sharpest tool in the box, but he had a heart the size of Belfast Lough. He was taking Mama, Dziadek and me out for the day. It was a fresh Sunday morning and Tata had said that it would stay dry all day, so Toni suggested that we would take a drive to Newcastle after church. Tata was doing a job for a friend of Mr Ferguson – Sunday or not, he was happy to take on extra work.

When Toni pulled up at our door I was actually looking forward to getting away. Besides, the following day was my birthday so I knew the day out was kind of in my honour.

We helped Dziadek fold himself into the front seat of the car, his spine curled, looking even frailer in the outside light. Mama and I climbed into the back.

'Should take us about forty-five minutes, or so,' Toni was saying, doing his one-handed-spinning-the-steering wheel thing. 'You'll love it, Dziadek – the Mourne Mountains come into view about seven or eight miles or so up the road. And further on, the Irish Sea. It'll be just like home.'

Dziadek nodded his head, but he didn't look convinced. Mama on the other hand was panting like an excited toddler. She hadn't been out of this city since we arrived in it nearly four years ago.

The Toyota climbed upwards out of Belfast, through little towns like Carryduff and Ballynahinch. Once you were out of the city everything was just so green. To be fair, Belfast wasn't a big city and you could see hills and mountains from almost every part of it, but out here was literally a breath of fresh air. Well, fresh air and passing whiffs of Toni's cheap aftershave and hair gel.

My brother talked non-stop for the whole journey, pointing out things as we drove along like a bloody tour guide.

'And round this corner we should get our first glimpse of Slieve Donard,' he was saying. 'It's the tallest mountain in the North of Ireland.'

'How do you know all this, son?' Mama asked, eyes wide with admiration.

'Tata and me, we have worked all over County Down. There are so many beautiful places.' He smiled, catching her eyes in the rear-view mirror. 'Wait till you see the beach at Newcastle, Ma. And Tollymore Forest. You'll think you're right back in Masuria!'

I noticed Dziadek grimace at this, as if in pain. Toni had moulded cushions around his limp body to make the journey more comfortable. This made him sit slightly forward, and he didn't seem to be looking out. In fact, his head never seemed to move. I was glad then of Toni's running commentary, because even if Dziadek couldn't see all around him, he could hear about it.

Over an hour later (not forty-five minutes!) we were entering the outskirts of Newcastle. Even though it was late September the town had a summer-holiday vibe about it. A huge old redbrick hotel stood at the top end of the promenade, looking out over the beach like some old Victorian sergeant major. We cruised down the main street with all its cafés and knick-knack shops and endless amusement arcades. Beyond us was the majestic Slieve Donard peak and for once Dziadek actually looked up.

'O rety!' he whimpered – oh my goodness! The wrinkles on his forehead creased into narrower frown lines. His rheumy eyes seemed brighter, like clear blue coins. 'That is one hell of a mountain!'

I don't know why but it made us laugh, Mama, Toni and me. It lightened all of us and by the time we'd found a parking space I was ready to jump out and enjoy the day – really enjoy the day. Toni had packed a wheelchair into the boot – apparently one of his customers had given it to him as his father no longer needed it – and Dziadek frowned and cursed about it for a bit, but he soon relented when he saw the length of the promenade. Toni threw a blanket over Dziadek's knees and off we went, dandering along like tourists, Toni beaming from ear to ear because he was doing everything right.

'How high is it, Antoni?' Dziadek asked, making Toni stop to look at the mountain again.

'It's 850 metres,' he answered, smug with pride. 'Impressive, isn't it?'

It was. Today it looked blue and purple and green and grey all rolled into one. It seemed to sweep right down towards the sea, just like 'The Mountains of Mourne' song said. Toni told us all about the views from the top: Scotland, the Isle of Man, Wicklow. He had learned all these things from customers, he said, and for once I felt proud of him. While I had moaned and groaned for the last few years, Toni had soaked up everything he could about his new country. Learning didn't just happen at Belview College and I realised I needed to remind myself of that.

'What is it, Dziadek?' I asked.

He was raising his hand up, like he was trying to reach something. Like he was trying to grab the mountain, age spots and scars and papery skin lining the back of his hand.

'Just trying to grab the image, Magda. Just trying to hold it so I can show it to your grandmother later.'

Toni, Mama and I exchanged glances but said nothing. Dziadek was smiling, so why ruin what was turning into a perfect day?

'Ice creams, anyone?' my big brother asked.

Toni had this day planned to a T.

'Why not?' I answered. If you couldn't have an ice creams the day before your birthday, then when could you?

Twenty minutes later we were slurping whipped ice cream like we'd never tasted the stuff before as we walked along the promenade. Mothers were sitting on the beach while little kids sieved and filtered sand through their fingers. Teenagers, maybe my age, maybe older, loped along in groups, giggling like they knew something I didn't, the girls swinging their long hair and snickering at the boys. I had never been part of a group like that in Ireland. Probably never would.

'*Hey, Maggie!*' a girl screeched out.

I looked over and saw Sophie, all luminous and glossy. What the heck?

'You didn't tell me you were coming to Newcastle today!' she scolded, like I was supposed to report my every move to her.

'Erm, we … just sort of decided … this morning,' I mumbled, painfully aware that I probably had ice cream all round my mouth.

The rest of the group stared at me and my family like we were a different species. I felt a prickle of heat burn right up into my cheeks.

'Cool!' Sophie declared, like I had just announced something amazing. 'This is Paul. Remember I told you about him?' She linked the tall boy's arm and gazed up at him like he was an Adonis. Which he kind of was – all bronzed and lithe and floppy dark hair. Except he wore a sneer on his face that made me feel two feet high.

'Hi there,' I said, just wanting to move on.

Mama was standing all wide-eyed and smiling, waiting to be introduced, and Toni was trying to look as cool as a person could while balancing an ice cream and pushing an old man in a wheelchair with a blanket draped round him.

'Hi, Toni,' Sophie squeaked, still clasping Sneer-boy. 'You're such a honey taking your grandfather out for the day. Oh, and this must be your mum?'

'Yeah – Mama, this is Sophie,' I said, sighing like it was painful to get the words out.

'Hell*ooo*,' my mum said, all emphasis in the wrong place.

'Gosh, it's so cool to meet you, Mrs Jankowska,' Sophie gushed, flicking her hair.

Sneer-boy snickered.

'Isn't Newcastle fab?' she went on. 'I cannot

believe we ran into you guys! Did you drive down in your new car, Toni?'

'Yeah, yeah,' Toni blustered.

New car? She knew the thing was an old banger! Now she was leaning down, smiling into my grandfather's face like he was a baby in a pram.

'Very nice to meet you, Mr Jankowski,' she said, sounding out each word like he might be deaf. He wasn't deaf – nor was he Mr Jankowski – but I was too mortified to point this out.

'Right, we'll get on then,' I muttered, starting to walk on. Drowning in embarrassment.

'Aw, not yet, Maggie. How do you fancy coming to Nugelato with us? Isn't it your big day tomorrow?' she asked, all sweetness and light.

I shook my head. 'No, it's OK. Thanks, Sophie.'

'You sure?' she asked, like I'd wounded her. 'Okey-dokey!' she said in a weird cowgirl sort of accent. 'See you tomorrow then, Mags!' She beamed, kissing me on the cheek. 'I'll bring your present to school in the morning.'

Mags? Cheek-kissing? I wanted the ground to swallow me up right there and then. Sneer-boy and the rest were still looking us up and down like we were from another planet. I knew what they were thinking – why would Sophie know somebody like me? I didn't have dip-dyed hair and a bust. I didn't wear short shorts and have big-slug eyebrows. No, I had jeans from Primark, hair scooped back in a plain ponytail, and trainers that a Polish friend of Mama's had passed on to me. No way would they have been seen in Nugelato with me!

We moved on.

'She seems nice, Magda,' Mama said, taking my hand like I was a child.

'Does she?' I replied.

I was in a huff now, sulking because we had run into Sophie and her gang, sulking because we were the uncoolest family in Northern Ireland, and sulking because I cared. The day was ruined. I couldn't care less after that about Toni's touristy facts, or the big old hotel named after the Slieve Donard. Even the ice cream felt stupid in my hand and I threw it into the next bin I came across.

'What is wrong, Magda?'

Poor Mama's face was furrowed with concern and the fact that she spoke in English nearly made me burst into tears. What could I say? That I hated being me? That I was ashamed of my Polishness and my Polish family? That even though my English was fluent some words still danced around in my head, mixed up.

'I just want to go home,' I coughed out in an angry sigh.

I knew I was being a little brat. I knew this day was for Mama and Dziadek as much as me, but I just wanted away from this town with its happy Sunday sightseers and gangs of cool kids. I could see Toni rolling his eyes and I knew that he could see right through me.

'What do you want to do, Dziadek?' he asked, bending down to my granddad, oblivious in his wheelchair.

'I too want to go home,' he answered, his eyes sweeping towards me.

The sky was starting to curdle into grey clouds anyway. A cooler breeze blew past us now and I felt justified – I was getting Dziadek home safely before the weather broke, like it always did in this blasted country. Yeah, it was nothing to do with embarrassment or jealousy – I was just thinking of Dziadek.

Toni turned the wheelchair and we all headed back to the car. Nobody spoke on the way home, not even Toni. But his eyes caught mine in the mirror more than once, and they were full of blame. And disappointment.

Chapter six

'Happy birthday, my little one,' Mama said, carrying a small package into the kitchen. It was wrapped in lilac tissue paper with a bow. I unpicked it and found the most gorgeous leather-bound notebook inside – not everybody's idea of the perfect thirteenth birthday present, but I was an absolute sucker for pretty stationery.

'I'm sorry it's so very little,' she went on, folding her arms around me. 'But I know you love to scribble away when you listen to Dziadek's stories. And now you can write some of your own.'

'Mama, I love it,' I said, hugging her back. 'It's perfect!'

'You want to invite your friend, Sophie, around

for a birthday cake after school?' she asked.

'No, it's OK, Mama. Just you and my family – it's fine.'

We always had a family birthday tea with Mum's homemade biscuit cake, made with butter, syrup and melted chocolate. Mama had taken the night off work especially and Tata and Toni had promised to be back in time.

'Now, go say good morning to Dziadek, then get ready for school, my love.'

I called out to Dziadek as I climbed the stairs, expecting a full-on hug and a birthday song. But when I opened his door he was pressing a tissue against a cut on his cheek.

'You OK, Dziadek?' I asked, going over to him.

He looked through me for a few seconds as if he didn't recognise me and then it was like his brain blinked back to normal. His hazy glaze disappeared and he threw his arms around me.

'Birthday girl!' he cried out. 'And now you are a teenager!'

'Did you cut yourself shaving, Dziadek?' I asked, reaching out to his face.

'Ah, these old hands aren't so steady any more, Magda. Nothing to worry about, my girl. Now, quickly – come over here!' he said, taking my hand away from his cheek and drawing me towards a big old chest underneath the window. 'I waited until you were thirteen,' he said excitedly. 'I know your grandmother would have wanted you to have this.'

He handed me something in a discoloured piece of cloth.

'Careful, Magda – don't break it.'

It was only loosely folded and when I pulled back the cloth there was a picture of my grandmother with a baby in her arms. Her hair was pulled tightly back from her face, accentuating her high cheekbones. She must have been close to sixty, but she was still beautiful. The baby seemed stiff and stern-faced in her arms.

'That is you, Magda – with my other Magda – two of my favourite girls,' he said proudly. 'Here, Granddaughter – it is yours.'

I let him take my hand and hold it tight, until my heart felt like it was being squeezed.

I looked closely at my *babcia* – my grandmother – and I could see how she tilted her chin up, just like I did.

'Thank you, Dziadek,' I said, tears stinging. 'I will treasure it.'

'Now run on, my girl, or you will be late for school.' He turned away from me in case I would see *his* tears and I backed out of the room.

The old photograph had a crack in the glass and

the frame was nothing special, but I knew I would treasure that gift. I took it to my room and placed it carefully on my bookshelf.

I grabbed my schoolbag and coat and shouted out a goodbye to Mama.

Outside, I ran for the bus, sending a silent prayer of thanks to whoever was up above that there was no stone-throwing this morning. Clearly birthdays were exempt.

Sophie bounced over as soon as I stepped inside the school foyer. 'Maggie, I can't wait to give you your present! But I'll wait until triple science. Mr Scott won't notice.' She pinched my cheek.

Seriously – did she think I was her pet or something?

'Your Toni looked *soo* fit yesterday,' she rabbited on, linking my arm as we walked to registration. 'Do you think he likes me?'

'Have you got a hormone imbalance or something, Sophie? How many boyfriends do you need?'

She cackled like she'd never heard anything so funny. 'Maggie, you have the best sense of humour *ever*! Anyway, Paul's not my boyfriend – he's just really *in*to me.' She rolled her eyes at the apparent boredom of it all. 'That's my old gang from my last school. Honestly, they just can't seem to get through a weekend without me.'

Where did you get confidence like that? Or was it arrogance? I searched her face for irony but, no, she was deadly serious.

After Miss Kennedy's usual monotonous 'rules for the day' we headed for the science block and parked ourselves on the back bench beside Anna.

Sophie couldn't wait to pull a parcel out of her bag, literally bouncing on the bench with excitement. Mr Scott was busy conferring with the lab technician and totally oblivious.

'Go on, go on! Open it!' she squeaked.

Anna watched from under her fringe, her eyes heavy with vague interest.

I put the package on the bench beside me to avoid drawing attention to it and unwrapped it carefully. Inside was a pencil drawing of my brother, clipped to a cardboard backing. He was standing beside his Toyota. Looking awkward and dorky. What the hell?

'Remember the photo I took on my phone? When you came to my house on Saturday? I sat up all last night doing this.'

For the second time in less than an hour I searched her face for sarcasm – was she taking the piss? The art work was brilliant, but Toni – Toni looked out of his depth, his hands loose by his sides and his podgy stomach protruding out of his jeans. And the bloody car looked exactly how it was – ancient and almost clapped out. I felt questions rattle through me.

'Why did you do this?' I asked her.

'Don't you like it, Maggie? Oh my God – I've got it wrong again, haven't I? Have I offended you? Do you think it's a crap drawing?' Her eyes were filling up with tears.

'No – it's just – why would you draw my brother? I don't get it.'

'It's a gift, Maggie. I – I thought you'd like it.'

Her voice had risen and now half the class was turning around to see what was going on.

'Well, I think it's really good,' Anna said, setting her words down carefully like well-chosen weapons, while looking disapprovingly at me under her brow.

Mia Campbell and two other girls were suddenly wrapped round us, gawking down at the picture and cackling with hilarity.

'Oh my God! Who *is* that?' Mia squealed, her high ponytail swinging like it had a life of its own.

'That's Maggie's brother,' Sophie said. 'I drew the picture for her birthday, but she doesn't like it.'

'But that's, like, *soo* ungrateful!' Mia sang out. 'I

60

mean, yeah, the guy looks like a dickhead but it's a brilliant picture. Magda, how can you be so mean to your friend? Like, if someone went to all that trouble for me I'd be *soo* made up.'

'I *am* grateful!' I said, my voice sounding high-pitched like a string instrument tightened. 'I just … well, it's not a very flattering picture, is it?'

Anna was now holding Sophie's hand and the rest of the class were out of their seats to enjoy the commotion. I felt the heat rise in my chest, tears pricking at my eyes. I had never *ever* wanted to be the focus of attention with these girls and now here I was, mired in their disapproving looks and hypocritical blabbering.

'I do like it, Sophie,' I said pointlessly. 'I'm sorry if you thought I didn't. It's … it's a great picture. Thank you.' My head hung in disgrace.

'You're just sayin' that now cos you know we all think you're an ungrateful bitch!' barked Chloe McKeever, all nasal and toxic.

'No, no, I'm not. I just didn't know what to make of it at first. I thought – I thought you were laughing at him, Sophie. Laughing at Toni – with this picture.'

Mia Campbell had her arm around a crying Sophie now, Anna's comforting hand displaced and Anna back to her role as dormouse in the corner.

'Why are you always so mean to me, Magda? I've

done nothing but try to be your friend,' Sophie panted out between sobs.

'I'm not mean, I'm j-j-just ... me,' I stuttered.

Filthy looks were thrown at me from every direction until Mr Scott came down to the back of the lab to break up the scrum.

'What's going on, girls?'

'Magda upset Sophie, sir!' Mia spat out.

Sophie's sobs now turned into full-blown hysterics and Mr Scott suggested that someone take her to the toilets to give her time to calm down.

'If you want to talk to your Year Head about whatever's troubling you, Sophie, I'm sure she'll be available after break,' Mr Scott said, deftly handing the problem over to someone else. 'Now the rest of us will get back to work. Right – Respiration. Open your text books at Page 30.'

The Belvies returned to their own benches, still casting cloudy looks at me over their shoulders. Anna put her elbow on the desk and rested her head in her hand, deliberately blocking me out. I put the picture in my bag and felt like crap, blinking rapidly to stop the tears from coming. What the heck had just happened? Did I get it all wrong? My throat suddenly felt that sharpness of supressed tears, like splinters of glass were stuck in it.

Sophie's eyes flashed at me when she came back,

and I knew that I had made a complete mess of things.

Mr Scott droned on about aerobic respiration and I felt cheated, angry. But there was something more in Sophie's eyes when she handed me that picture. I just knew there was.

I felt like a leper on the bus home that afternoon. Not that any of my schoolmates ever sat or stood with me anyway but, instead of just ignoring me today, they were scowling at me. And, just to top the day off, the shop wall below our flat had fresh red paint splattered all over it – FORENERS OUT! The artist had obviously paid *loads* of attention in Literacy lessons.

The smell of melted butter and syrup was wafting right down the stairs. In the kitchen, Mama was stirring away feverishly with a wooden spoon and humming to herself.

There was just about room for a table and five chairs in our small kitchen, the fifth chair being a plastic garden one Tata had rescued from a garden he had worked on in Bangor. That was my seat. If I pulled it over to the small window at the side of the kitchen I could see endless rows of red-bricked houses and occasional graffiti. And if I stood on the chair on tiptoe I could just about see Divis Mountain

63

and the Black Mountain towering over the northwest of the city. Toni had told me that there used to be a British Army barracks there, back when 'The Troubles' were on. He had told me all about Nationalists and Unionists and how some of them had hated each other.

'Not all of them, Magda. Lots of people here didn't want the hate. Now it is better,' he'd added, full of his own wisdom.

'Yeah, now they hate *us* instead of each other,' I'd muttered back.

'No, Magda – just like before – not all of them hate,' he'd argued. 'People Tata and I have worked for have been very good. And the people I meet at the car rallies – they too are very good.'

I sometimes wished I saw things through Toni's eyes instead of being cursed with cynicism. No-one else in my family seemed cynical. It was just Miserable Magda with all the negative vibes.

'Do you think the Troubles will come back, Toni?' I had asked him then, trying to make up for my snarling pessimism.

'No, Magda. The Good Friday Agreement made sure of that. Belfast is booming. And the Jankowski family is here to reap the rewards!' He laughed, all gap-toothed and believing.

I didn't know what the Good Friday Agreement

was, and I cared even less, but it was another time when I realised that Toni had knowledge that he hadn't found in books. He had found it through living life. Maybe I was too much like Dziadek: cloistered away in Belview College by day and drowning in Polish memories in my grandfather's room by night.

'Here are your father and brother,' Mama said now, peering through the kitchen window before turning to the table and setting out a huge plate of cheese and mushroom *pierogi* – dumplings.

Even though *pierogi* were my favourite snack *ever*, I was depressed again, thinking about the crap morning I'd had.

Tata and Toni burst in to the kitchen looking pleased with themselves, one an older version of the other. If they saw the message on the wall, they were doing a good job of ignoring it.

'Here you are, my little Magda!'

'*Open it, open it!*' Toni yelled like a toddler.

This was my fourth package of the day and I secretly dreaded what would be inside it after the shame of Sophie's present. It was a Sheaffer pen, cradled in a little plastic case and it was perfect! I hugged them both and resolved that today would be the day I learned to be positive and embrace life. I was thirteen now – time to girl-up, or whatever.

But that was before Tata's big announcement, and then I was right back to Square One.

'Tomorrow we start in your school, Magda,' he said, pulling his chair out and settling himself down at the table. 'It is very a good job,' he went on, in English. 'Toni and I are very lucky. We will show them our skills and be *indispensable.*' He rolled his tongue around the last word and it pained me that my dad could teach at Belview College instead of mowing the bloody lawns. 'We will be able to keep an eye on our little girl.' He winked, before taking a dumpling in his hand and tucking in. '*Mmm*, Katarina. These are perfect!' He smiled at Mama as if life was perfect. Dumplings and grass-cuttings – what else did a man need?

'Has anyone called Papa?' Mama asked.

I pushed my chair back and left to get Dziadek, sick to the stomach at the thought of Mia, Chloe and the rest of their crew laughing at my father and brother the following day. And every day after that. My innocent, happy, guileless father and brother – they had no clue how horrible Belfast girls could be. Belfast *privileged* girls, anyway. The smell of *pierogi* was now making my insides heave. When did the best of Poland become the worst of Ireland?

Chapter seven

My bedroom window faced east, so there was no sunset to be seen there. But I could see the clouds and Belfast's silhouette. Modern high-rise buildings mixed with rusty Victorian. All around me were homes, offices, lives, cars moving and the streetlights as orange as fire. There was one stray dog wandering along the main street, moving slow and low.

My birthday had been a disaster! Even Mama and Tata had lost patience with me when I'd refused the biscuit cake and gone to bed. I'd said I felt sick, and in a way I did. Sick of all this. Sick of trying to fit in. Sick of pretending. I folded my arms and looked out across the evening sky. When would Belfast ever feel like home?

'Magda?' It was Mama's voice. Soft as the rain that had started outside.

She opened the door and came in, standing behind me with her arms around my waist. She tucked her head against mine, smelling of talcum powder. Apparently, talcum powder was the next best thing to shampoo, according to my mum. She loved thick body creams and scented talc.

'What is it, Magda?'

I curled my head into hers and let myself cry.

'I don't know, Mama. I just feel … on the edge of everything. Like I don't fit in.'

'Little one, we all feel like that,' she purred in my ear. 'Since coming here to Ireland, I walk on boundaries. Does that make sense?'

I nodded.

'We live what we live, and we make the best of it. I know you are angry with us for leaving Poland. And I know you are angry with your Polishness too. But, Magda, that is so wrong. And so upsetting for the rest of your family. Don't walk on the edges of life like you are some kind of embarrassment, Magda. Climb right in and make the most of it. After all, you only have one chance to live.'

And with that she kissed me on the cheek, the softest, warmest kiss in the world. And I knew I'd been a complete bitch to everyone.

'Mama, I don't feel well,' I whimpered. 'Can I stay off school tomorrow?' I turned round and gazed up at her like the two-year-old I felt inside.

'But, Magda – you have never missed a day of school. Ever!'

'Please, Mama. Just tomorrow. Until my stomach settles.'

She looked right through me and I knew she understood.

'Just one day, Magda. Stay with me, stay with your grandfather.' She nodded her head like it was a cure. 'Then back to school to your learning. I know how you love it.'

I felt like a parcel, wrapped in her arms. She was still wearing her white apron, her hair loosely twisted into a plait. Mama wasn't even forty yet, but sometimes she acted like she had existed forever. She didn't have Sophie's mum's trendy bob or elegant job, but she was there for us, through thick and thin.

I undressed, put on my pyjamas and she tucked me into bed like a small child, kissed me on the forehead and told me everything would be OK. If only.

Chapter eight

'Come on, Dziadek. Let's go to Botanic Gardens,' I suggested the next morning. 'You too, Mama.'

Since Toni had brought the wheelchair back, Dziadek no longer needed to be stuck in the flat. Toni had it parked at the bottom of the stairs, just inside the front door.

'You are feeling better, Magda?' my mum asked with one raised eyebrow.

'Just a little, Mama. The fresh air will be good for my tummy. And for Dziadek.'

She rolled her hair back into a loose bun and nodded her head. Knowingly.

Mama and I got ready and helped Dziadek into his coat. We got him down the stairs with some difficulty and sat him in the chair. Mama tucked his blanket around him, and I pushed him into the shop. He liked to go through the shop now and again for a chat with Michal. I was praying for a stone-free morning and, by the time they'd had their natter, it was nearly ten o'clock, so the chances were that we were safe from the missile-messengers by now. They had probably left for school or work, or whatever they did in between stone-throwing episodes.

The autumn sky was still slightly dimmed but a small bit of sun spilled down on to the Belfast pavements. Mama hurried along beside me, checking every minute or so to see if Dziadek was warm enough. There was a cold-weather smell this morning, despite the little bit of sunlight: the smell of smoke and dried leaves on the city streets. Dziadek had been a gardener in his previous life and Tata had picked up everything he knew from him – when he had switched careers. Tata had gone from teacher of geography to seed-planter, but Dziadek had always loved the earth, and Botanic Gardens was the nearest thing we had to remind him of that. 'I am a planter,' he used to say, back in Poland. 'I reap what I sow.' He used to laugh when he said this, like it was the most profound statement in all of Masuria.

I had persuaded Dziadek to go on the Easibus

with spaces inside for disabled passengers and within minutes we were outside the gardens and the Ulster Museum. Queen's University students were already sauntering in and out of the park, and mums with babies in strollers were ambling along, phones in one hand, handles of pushchairs in the other. We took the path for the Palm House first, pushing Dziadek along the walkway bordered by old oaks and conifers, smelling the pine and fresh air as we went. Dziadek loved the displays of colour in the Palm House, rattling off names like geranium, fuchsia and begonia – the names are the same in Polish of course but pronounced differently. Mama held one of his hands as we walked along. I knew the Belvies would be immersed in Art class by now with Miss Price, but I was trying really hard not to think about them. Mia and Sophie were probably BFFs by now and good luck to them – it was bound to happen sooner or later. Right now, I was happy in the park with my family.

'Dahlias!' Dziadek called out suddenly, pointing to some crimson-coloured flowers along the borders of the park. 'So hard to grow them in Masuria,' he sighed.

'Why, Dziadek?'

'Too much clay in our soil, Magda – all the lakes, you see,' he said, spreading his hands on his knees.

The pale skin hung from them like it was melting. 'Land of a thousand lakes, they call it,' he breathed. 'But you know that already, little one.'

I did, but I still liked to hear him talk about home like it was some kind of fairy tale. The truth was, life back in Poland *hadn't* been a fairy tale, but I wasn't about to point that out. Tata had lost his job and that had meant losing our house. Not that our poky Belfast flat felt like the height of luxury, but apparently our circumstances were improving every day, according to Mama. It was just a pity that that improvement involved my father and brother working in *my school*!

'So how about the museum now?' Mama asked.

Dziadek nodded, always a sucker for a free museum visit. Mama pushed him up the short hill towards the museum with its 'white neo-classical façade' (according to Toni) at one end and the bare modernist bit at the other. Toni had told me that the modern end was an example of Brutalist architecture because it was all raw concrete and rugged. (I had agreed with him that it was definitely brutal all right!) Toni was infatuated with the animals and plants and fossils in the Nature Zone of the museum and spent half of his Sunday afternoons roaming around it. Like I said, the free entry was a *big* attraction for our family. Me, I liked the history of people best. My family thought it was beyond weird, but I could look at Takabuti all day long. She was over two thousand five hundred years old and, to be honest, she looked it – all black-faced and wizened, with one skinny hand and one skinny foot hanging out of the linen bandages. Once mistress of a great house in Egypt, now she was one of the most looked-at women in Northern Ireland. There was no accounting for taste in this corner of the world! Someone called Thomas Gregg had brought her to Belfast nearly two hundred years ago and, apparently, she had been a sensation!

'Where to first?' Mama asked Dziadek as we walked into the huge Welcome Zone – all white space and light. Square black sofas rested in the middle, empty today bar one woman with a toddler to one side of her and a baby resting on her chest.

'Living World,' he breathed.

Mama wheeled him into the lift and off we went to the Nature Zone on the third floor. An open corridor led to this section, with a skeleton of a triceratops menacing on one side and poor Peter the Polar Bear on the other. Poor Peter was about 30 years old when he had died at Belfast Zoo – another Toni teaser! – and he had been stuffed and moved to the Ulster Museum during The Troubles over forty years before.

'He made terrible noises as they transported him,

Magda,' Toni had told me. 'Gas noises from decomposing. And the noises continued through that first night in the museum so the night-watchman called the police. In those days in Belfast any suspicious noises would have scared the living daylights out of people! Then the press was all over it, calling it the Rampage of the Dead Bear. It was all over the worldwide news!'

But, looking at Peter now, all I could think about was how he had been enclosed in such a small enclosure in life – and then stuffed to the gills in death. It just didn't seem right.

Mama, Dziadek and I went straight to the Living World section to look at minerals and crystals of all shapes and colours, from creamy quartz to amethyst to malachite.

'Your birthstone, Katarina,' Dziadek pointed out to my mum.

I always thought that the rich violet amethyst suited Mama perfectly, and she always wore a little pearl-drop shape of it on a chain around her neck. It was supposed to represent courage and that's something my mum had in bucketloads. She faced everything that life threw at her and kept on smiling. Maybe it was something to do with being born in February in freezing-cold Masuria.

'Remember when we bought you that necklace,

Katarina? For your eighteenth birthday?' He nodded at her amethyst stone. 'Your grandmother had very good taste, Magda, as you can see from her choice of husband!' He laughed, his eyes watery blue. 'I miss her,' he said then, shaking his head. 'I want to go home to her.'

He hung his head and suddenly the oxygen seemed to drain from Mama and me. We were never too sure just how much Dziadek was in the present or the past.

'Babcia's back in Poland, Dziadek,' I said softly. 'You scattered her ashes over your favourite lake, remember?'

'Of course I remember!' he grunted back to me, his moods these days as changeable as the Irish weather. 'I know where I laid my own wife to rest, Magda. Don't patronise me!'

Mama must have seen the shock on my face because she knelt down straight away to soothe him. 'Magda wasn't patronising you, Papa. She was just trying to help you to remember.'

'You all think I am a crazy old man!' he shouted, banging his weak fist on his knee. 'I know where my wife is, and I know where I want to be. *Beside her!* In Masuria. Take me home!'

His voice was weakening, but it still caught the attention of onlookers. I could see them watching us, puzzling about this weird family speaking in a weird language, with the weird old man in the wheelchair crying like a baby, tears dropping from him like our leaky tap in the kitchen.

'Come on, Magda. We will take him home,' Mama said, turning his wheelchair around sharply.

'*Not Belfast!*' he was shouting. '*Home!*' His chest was rising and falling like an inflatable cushion.

Mama was nearly in tears too, punching in G for Ground Floor in the lift, her fingers trembling.

As soon as we were outside I felt myself breathe again, but Dziadek was still hacking away with sobs. I was ashamed at myself for being embarrassed. I was ashamed that I even cared what onlookers thought of us in the museum.

There would be no Takabuti today – that much was obvious.

On the street, city buses bustled past and university students at Queen's strode backwards and forwards across the road. In less than ten minutes we got off another Easibus and were back at our flat, just minutes away from university life and yet miles away in culture. Or lack of it. Unless you counted the graffiti and the aversion to foreigners.

Mama thought it was best to let Dziadek sleep for a while and, after we managed to get him up the stairs and settled down, he sank into his wing-backed chair by the window and fell into a deep slumber. For a minute or two we both watched him, his gaunt face as pale as Takabuti's bandages. He looked a little more peaceful now as his chin dropped and his breathing slowed into a rhythm – the slow thumping of his aged heart.

'I think he's finding it harder and harder to be away from Poland,' Mama said later as we sat in the kitchen. 'Maybe I made a mistake, Magda. Maybe I should never have brought him here to Ireland.'

'Don't upset yourself, Mama. You thought you were doing the right thing,' I said.

She slumped forward on the table, her head in her hands. I went and wrapped my arms around her. She still smelt of talcum powder and as I leaned my head into her neck I felt that familiar warm softness that I would never, ever stop loving. My mum put everyone else before herself – everyone – and the thought that she had somehow wronged Dziadek was eating away at her.

'Maybe we could take him back for a holiday, Mama? At Christmas, maybe?' I suggested, realising as soon as I spoke that he was way too weak for such a journey and, anyway, Christmas was the most expensive time of the year for travelling.

Mama nodded, returned my hug and cried into

my shoulder. 'It's a good idea, Magda, but I don't think it is possible,' she whimpered. 'We must try to keep him happy here. That's all we can do.'

She said it like it was a temporary thing – like Dziadek wouldn't be around for much longer. I was just trying to process this when, through the open door, I heard Tata call up the stairs.

'We're home!' he was singing out in English. *'And we've got company!'*

Mama and I glanced at each other, puzzled. Apart from Michal, the shop owner, hardly anyone ever called. Mama, Tata and Toni had got to know people in Belfast, but they had never formed the kind of friendships that involved calling at each other's homes. They met at church or exchanged pleasantries in the shop, but that was about it.

Tata pushed through the kitchen door and held out his left arm in introduction.

'Look who's come to see you, Magda!' he trumpeted.

Coming in behind him, looking all glossy and meek, was a shy, smiling Sophie, looking at me through long lashes, like butter wouldn't melt.

Chapter nine

'I was so worried when you weren't at school today, Maggie,' she said. 'Anna said that you've never missed a single day, so I thought you must be really ill or something!'

Toni and Tata stood there looking at her, like some sort of angel from heaven had landed in the middle of our tiny kitchen. All prim and pristine in her uniform, long chestnut hair cascading down her back, she looked completely out of place. We all stood there like a bloody tableau until Mama had the sense to invite her to sit down.

'Can I get you something to drink, Sophie?' she asked.

'No, I'm fine, Mrs Jankowska,' she answered

sweetly. 'I just came to check on Maggie. I missed her today in school.'

She beamed at me like I was her favourite puppy. Didn't she remember yesterday? The day when I was cast as the evil villain and she was the poor damsel in distress?

'Why don't you two go to your room, Magda?' Mama said, obviously thinking this was what normal teenage girls did. But Belview Babes didn't have bedrooms the size of a linen cupboard.

'No, it's OK, we'll just go for a walk,' I mumbled, eager to get Sophie out of there. Even if it did mean strolling along Missile Street! I grabbed my jacket and nodded at her to follow, cringing with every step I took down the narrow staircase.

'How cool to live above a shop!' she cooed, glancing through the other door that led into Michal's place.

I could tell that she wanted to go in, to *ooh* and *aah* her way around the quaint Polish delicacies – as she would probably call them. I pushed through the outer door and onto the street without even answering.

As soon as I turned onto the main street I saw a huddle of boys with hands in their pockets, sneering in our direction.

'So?' Sophie said, catching up with me.

'So what?' I answered, huddling into my jacket.

'How come you weren't at school today? I was worried about you.'

Was she *really* that dumb?

'Sophie, I was mortified yesterday! I couldn't face school today because ... because I'm bloody Harley Quinn and Poison Ivy rolled into one!'

'What do you mean?' she asked, her forehead creased into a frown.

'Bloody hell, Sophie – you were *there*, remember? The picture? You crying? The other girls?'

'A bit of bitch-fighting!' one of the sneery hoodies guffawed. 'My money's on the looker!'

'Nah, that feckin' foreign one could take her any day!' Hoody Number 2 grunted back.

Hoody Number 3 said nothing.

I shoved past them and smelt their stinking smoky breaths. One of them *miaowed* at Sophie. Seriously!

'But that's all forgotten about, Maggie. You didn't like my picture – that's fine. No big deal.' She shrugged, eyes wide, like nothing had happened.

'Of *course* it's a big deal. You were crying, remember? The Belview Bitches moved in and my head was on the stake!'

'But I cry at the drop of a hat, Maggie. It's no biggy!' She laughed. 'And since when did you care what Mia and the others think of you?'

She had a point, but she was making this whole thing seem way too simple. I couldn't shake the thought that she had somehow set me up with that picture of Toni. Maybe I was just paranoid.

'You didn't come to school today because you thought everyone was mad at you?' she said, the penny finally dropping.

'*Duh* – yeah,' I answered.

'But that's so lame, Maggie. And so *not* like you.' She linked my arm and kissed me on the cheek. 'We're BFFs, remember?'

'That's better, girls!' Hoody Number 1 jeered after us. 'A bit of girl-on-girl!' he cackled.

Sophie turned round and gave him one of her biggest smiles. Followed by a two-fingered gesture that made the creeps whoop with pleasure. Well, two of them anyway. Hoody Number 3 didn't seem so sure of himself.

'Let's get away from here,' I said, pulling her towards the city centre where we would hopefully lose the prats.

We walked as far as Belfast City Hall and parked ourselves on a bench in the grassy area beside it. I huddled further into my coat and decided I would try to explain.

'That picture of Toni – you must have seen how it made him look,' I said, softening a bit.

'It made him look like Toni,' she answered with a shrug. 'I hope. Unless my art work's *really* off!'

Not for the first time I found myself really looking at her, trying to work her out. Her grey-blue eyes stared right back at me, guileless.

'Can we forget about it, now? You've *got* to come back to school tomorrow,' she gushed. 'We've got another double period of our Homes and Houses project to work on with Miss Price. *And* we have a new form teacher!'

'Where's Miss Kennedy gone?' I asked, actually finding myself interested.

'Don't know, but we were told that she won't be back until *after Christmas*!' she said, linking my arm again. 'Do you think she's having a baby?'

I thought of Miss Kennedy's concave stomach and thought it was highly unlikely. She didn't seem like the kind of person to get sick, but there was obviously something wrong with her if she was going to be off for over two months.

The city centre was starting to empty itself of office workers and shoppers. City Buses pulled up and pulled out from their stops on Donegall Square, taking workers to the suburbs and beyond, while the red sightseeing buses were carrying fewer and fewer tourists with the dropping dusk. Royal Avenue up ahead was beginning to shut down for the night and the city had a feeling of winding down, loosening up. Maybe I could give that a go myself.

'So, my granddad, Mama and I went to Botanic Gardens today,' I said, trying to offer a few crumbs of friendship. 'We didn't get as far as Takabuti though. Granddad became a bit upset ...' I tailed off.

'*Takabuti!*' she shrieked. 'I love Takabuti! We have *soo* much in common, Maggie!' She squeezed my arm again, grinning into my face like I had the answers to the universe written all over me. What did she *see* when she looked at me?

'Let's go again at the weekend,' she gushed. 'We said we'd do Botanic anyway, didn't we? Do you think anyone really knows who Takabuti was?'

'She lived in Thebes, she was married and died somewhere between the ages of twenty and thirty,' I reeled off. 'I guess that's as much as we need to know.'

'Yeah, but don't you wonder what she was like – what kind of person she was?' Sophie asked, going all American-accented again.

'Of course I do,' I answered. 'But no-one really knows, so I just let myself imagine.'

'Go on then – spill. What does the great Magda Jankowska imagine?'

I felt shy about telling her the secret life of Takabuti

that I had stored in my mind. I had a whole world going on in there, not just about Takabuti but all kinds of things – a kind of separate universe where I wasn't Mopey Maggie in the corner, but a talented writer full of ideas and plans and passion. Stories I stored away like sweets in a jar. So, I started to tell her about Lady Takabuti and her palatial home along the Nile, writing on her clay tablet while servants took care of her children and home. Her deep, dark eyes and secret desires. Her rows with her father, Nespare, and her close bond with her mother, Tasenirit. Her love of the lyre and her distaste for beer.

'Beer? What was she doing drinking beer?' Sophie laughed, her nose crinkling up.

'*Duh* – because you couldn't risk drinking the water – it might not be clean,' I giggled back, enjoying myself now.

'Do you think she was happy?' Sophie probed.

'Who knows?' I answered. 'She died young, we know that much.'

'Have you got a bucket list, Maggie?' Sophie asked, all bright-eyed.

'A what?'

'A bucket list – you know, things you want to do before you *kick the bucket*. Die!'

'Bloody hell, Sophie, I'm not planning on dying any time soon! I'm a bit young to have a bucket list!'

'Yeah – but if you did?'

I took a deep breath and thought. I had plans and goals for the rest of my life, but a bucket list? Things I really, really wanted to do before the ever-after? To be accepted, I thought. To be on the inside instead of the outside. But I didn't say that to Sophie – I just shrugged and mumbled something about writing a book one day. Writing a story that people would actually read, with *my* name on the front cover. Sophie blathered something about that being a brilliant thing to have on a bucket list and then practically salivated about how she was going to marry someone with a title and be Lady Such-and-Such and live on a big estate. The only estates I knew in Belfast were sprawling housing estates, each dwelling looking just like the next one, but I had a feeling she had something different in mind.

'Ben says I should marry for money,' she stated matter-of-factly. 'The love will come afterwards.'

'Seriously?' I asked. 'Your dad said that?'

'He sure did. My dad always gives good advice.'

'But, is that advice not a bit … skewed? What about your mum and dad? Didn't they marry for love?'

'Of course they did, that's the problem. They married with their hearts, not their heads. Now look at the two of them – 10,000 miles apart!' Her grey-blue eyes looked cold, flinty. Sparkly Sophie's shine had disappeared again.

'Listen, why don't we head back? We'll be packed like sardines in our tiny kitchen but you're welcome to stay for dinner.'

'Really? Oh, Maggie, that would be lovely,' she said, her mouth splitting into a huge grin.

I was reasonably sure she'd been invited back to lots of other friends' homes for dinner – bigger, better homes with proper *Belfast* food – but she did seem pretty pleased to be invited to ours. If she was faking it, she was bloody good at it. Big, fat drops of rain started to fall on us as we walked back along the shiny streets. They came at us, sudden and hard as stones. We started to run, laughing through the downfall, splashing rainwater onto our legs as we ran past the infamous Europa Hotel (the 'most bombed hotel in Europe') and up to Shaftesbury Square. There was no sign of the hoodies as we charged towards the front door.

Panting and wet, we raced up the stairs and into the flat.

Our small kitchen was warm with steam. The table in the centre with its nutbrown tablecloth was already set for six people so Mama must have expected Sophie back.

'*Czesc, dziewczyny!*' Mama said, beginning to

ladle *krupnik* soup into bowls. Then she repeated in English, 'Hello, girls!'

'Will I call Dziadek?' I asked, turning already towards the stairs up to the attic.

'No, I'll just take this up to him on a tray, Magda. He's not feeling up to joining us.'

I caught the worry in her eyes before she blinked it away.

Tata pulled a chair out for Sophie and he took the smaller plastic one.

'No, Mr Jankowski, you sit here. I'm happy to sit on the garden chair,' Sophie protested, standing up again.

'Not way,' Tata answered, getting his *not* and his *no* mixed up. 'You are our guest – please, sit down on this proper seat.'

Sophie reached to tuck a stray hair behind her ear and sat down dutifully, smiling. Soon she was gushing about the food.

'This soup looks absolutely gorgeous!' she sang out as Mama came back down the stairs. 'What did you say it was called, Mrs Jankowska?'

'*Krupnik*,' answered Mama. 'It is a kind of barley soup with chicken and vegetables.'

She brought some wheaten bread to the table – one of our few concessions to Irish food – and sat down beside Toni.

'Mama usually uses onions and carrots and

whatever she's got in, basically, for the *krupnik*,' I explained. 'And potatoes, of course!' I laughed, rolling my eyes at Toni and Tata.

'Potatoes are sacred,' Toni said, smiling at Sophie. 'No meal is complete without them.'

It was nice actually. The flat was warm, my family were smiling round the table, the food was good. Maybe I should have had the courage to invite people back before. What had I been so ashamed of?

Sophie was the perfect guest – suitably polite and confident enough to ask the right questions, feigning an interest in flowerbeds and soil. Tata asked her about school and which subjects she enjoyed. Toni bigged himself up, talking about cars and engines, which was about as interesting as algebra, but whatever. I didn't mind. Sophie's face was flushed with warmth and she seemed to be enjoying herself. We were an unlikely pair, but maybe she did actually like being around me.

Mam was smiling at her family, her cheekbones shiny in the light. But there was a thinness to her smile and I knew she was thinking about Dziadek.

'Oh, I forgot to tell you, Maggie!' Sophie burst out. 'There's a special assembly tomorrow – it's the anniversary of the school, or something, and they were looking for volunteers to do things, you know, like readings and stuff.'

'Oh yeah, we always shut down the timetable for the morning on that date. Strange that Miss Kennedy hadn't been preparing us for it sooner.'

'Yeah, well, maybe she forgot. Anyway, our new form teacher, Mr Mawhinney, was trying to get it sorted this morning. So I volunteered you, Maggie, to read one of your stories.'

She said it like it was the most natural thing in the world, like Magda Jankowska stood up at assembly all the time and read aloud. In her Polish accent, with her voice faltering and her limbs shaking. Like she'd ever be picked to do *anything* of such importance.

'You *what*?' I asked, quick as a whip.

'I … I thought you'd like that. You want to be an author –' She broke off, her voice snapping like a twig.

'What a lovely idea!' Tata said, nodding at Sophie and then at me, warning me with his eyes to be gracious.

'But you know I can't do that! Won't do that. What the heck, Sophie?' Was she pure dumb or was this some sort of set-up? Again?

'Magda, please don't speak like that. Sophie is our guest!' Mama was flapping, embarrassed at my outburst.

'But why would a friend do that? Why do you

keep embarrassing me, Sophie?' I said, throwing my spoon down on the table.

Sophie's face had gone white.

'Why are you so bloody clueless?' I was almost crying now.

'Magda, do not behave like this!' Tata said angrily. 'Apologise to your friend immediately!'

Sophie smiled thinly at me, but my throat felt rusted up. I couldn't apologise because I couldn't speak. The thought of standing up on that stage tomorrow was jabbing at my stomach like a cramp. I turned and ran out of the room and down onto Missile Street for the second time that evening, hunching into myself against the rain and crying with shame. Sophie Long had me as mixed-up as a trick-or-treat bucket and I just didn't know whether she was stupid – or downright malicious.

Chapter ten

It was only mizzling outside now, but the temperature seemed to have dropped since I'd been inside. Windows glinted along Radlan Street, squares of light shining out at me like sneering smiles. Were the families inside those houses happy? Did they contain teenagers who didn't snap with tension every five minutes, or run away from the dinner table like a toddler having a tantrum? I felt *so*, so stupid. Stupid for blowing up like that and stupid for getting Sophie wrong. *Every. Single. Time.* I would be the ungrateful Polish bitch – again – and she would be Princess Perfect. Why the heck did I tell her about my stories? I should have kept my big mouth shut.

There was a rundown play park nearby where

you'd see small kids playing sometimes. I figured I might as well go there as anywhere else. The toes of my trainers were dark from wet grass by the time I sat down on the solitary swing. The ground below it was sunken and muddy, and I could hardly reach it with my feet. I sat, clutching the chains and rocking slightly back and forth until I sensed there was somebody else – somebody behind me. I swung round and saw a grey hood and my stomach sank. Not again!

'*Spierdalaj!*' I screamed. (You can probably guess what that means in English!)

I was sick and tired of prats in hoods and sick and tired of being the Bitch of Belfast. Why couldn't I just have a normal day without demented granddads and shifty Sophies? My heart was breaking in two over Dziadek and my head was all over the place about my *frenemy* back in the kitchen. Mama and Tata's looks of disappointment were etched on my brain and I just wanted to tell the whole world to bugger off.

The hoody shuffled towards me and I swear I was ready to reach out and belt him one.

'*Can't you leave me alone?*' I shouted.

He stopped short, hunched, looking at me from under thick, black brows. I recognised him as Hoody 3 – the quiet one.

'I'm sorry,' he said, his voice so low I barely heard him. His lips didn't even seem to have moved.

'Sorry for what?' I growled.

'For my mates. What they do.'

'What are you on about?' Jesus, why couldn't he just go away and let me be miserable?

'My mates – they give you a hard time,' he said, scuffing one foot on the grass, his hands so deep in his pockets the hoody was stretched right down.

'You're apologising?'

He nodded, scuffing the other foot now.

I couldn't help it, I burst out laughing. What the heck was going to happen next on this crazy day? The other two hoodies would turn up with a bunch of flowers for me?

His face went from grey to red, blushes creeping up into his cheeks.

'Why?' I asked him. 'Why are you apologising?'

He shrugged a shoulder, pulled up his bottom lip like he didn't know the answer, still scuffing.

'If you don't like what they do, why do you hang around with them?'

Another shrug. 'Cos they let me,' he said.

'*Let* you?'

He nodded. 'Nobody else does.'

Bloody hell, was this turning into a counselling session? Was I supposed to tell him that he should value himself more than this, not let himself be used by prats like them? But who was I to talk? I wanted to blend in as much as he did.

'What's your name?'

'Colin,' he mumbled, inching closer. 'What's yours?'

'Maggie.'

'Why are you out here in the rain, Maggie?'

'Cos I seem to have pissed everyone off at home,' I answered, thinking that my vocabulary seemed to have taken a turn for the worst in the last ten minutes. 'Why are *you* out here in the rain?'

'Cos there's nobody at home to piss off.'

He sort of smiled at this, showing sharp, yellow teeth. He did some sort of shuffling thing, turned a half-circle and then took his hands out of his pockets.

'Are you hungry?' he asked.

'No. Are you?'

'A bit,' he answered, glancing over at a lone chip van on the edge of the park.

'Come on, then,' I said, leaping off the swing and landing beyond the muddy hollow.

He hovered behind me and as we reached the chip van I realised that I was the one expected to do the buying.

'Just a chip?' I asked him, hoping that I had enough change in my pocket.

He nodded and I handed over a pound. A man

wearing a leather jacket and a baseball cap handed over chips in a polystyrene container, the steam coming off them like a fog.

'You want salt and vinegar?' I called over my shoulder.

He nodded. A hoody of few words.

After dousing them in both, I handed them over to him.

'No, they're yours,' he said, shaking his head. 'I'll just share.'

'But I got them for you ...' I started.

But then I realised that that wasn't the deal. That would make him look like a complete scrounger – this way at least he could just cadge a few chips and keep some self-respect. So, I held on to the chips and walked along, Mr Hoody beside me, waiting patiently to be offered.

'So why have your mates got it in for *foreigners*?' I asked, stretching out the word like it was dirty. I blew on a hot, fat chip and popped it into my mouth, relishing its lovely soft mushiness.

'Cos they're afraid of them,' he answered.

'Why?'

'Cos my mates are dumb. Anything they don't know about or understand, they're afraid of.'

'They're *good* friends of yours, then?' I said, grinning.

'Nah, they're just lads I hang around with. Dumb lads,' he added with a smile.

'So who did they terrorise before we moved in?'

'A Chinese family. They're fair like that – they don't pick and choose which foreigners they hate, they just hate all of them.'

I caught a sparkle in his eye and I wondered where this Colin had come from. He wasn't stupid – he just acted like he was.

We were walking past some sort of youth club place now. Its roof was circled with barbed wire and someone had painted FORENERS OUT in white paint on the wall, using the same 'phonetic' spelling they had used on our building. There were some older kids standing smoking in the doorway, watching us.

'Maybe you should get back,' Colin said.

'Maybe.'

'And don't speak to anyone until you're back on the main road,' he mumbled, starting to walk away from me.

I knew what he was trying to say – don't speak so they won't know you're foreign. I thought, not for the first time, how weird it was that people could understand unspoken words, no matter what language they were in.

I started to wander back in the direction of home,

glancing round once to see Colin disappear into an alleyway through a sea of red-bricked houses.

My heart started thumping in my chest again at the thought of facing everyone back at the flat. I knew I'd be in big trouble with Mama and Tata – they hated bad manners and hated tantrums even more. And how could I justify myself? Telling them that I thought Sophie might be a secret *frenemy* would make no sense to them whatsoever. I could just imagine the look of disappointment on their faces. My parents were brought up to see the good in everyone – Toni was the same. I seemed to be the only cynic in our family and I hated myself for it.

I braced myself as I turned the key in the door, ready to make a full apology to everyone.

Only Mama was there.

'Where's Sophie?' I asked.

'Your father and Toni have taken her home.'

Mama was sitting on the two-seater sofa, reading a Polish newspaper, her glasses perched on the end of her nose. I always thought it made her look older when she wore them.

'I'm sorry, Mama,' I said, sitting on the edge of the sofa and curling my head into her shoulder.

She didn't answer.

'Mama?'

She shook her head. 'I don't want to talk, Magda.'

Oh God, this was worse than a scolding!

'Oh, Mama, please don't fall out with me.'

More shaking of the head. 'Go to your room, Magda. Your father and I will speak to you tomorrow.' She didn't lift her eyes away from the page in front of her.

My stomach felt like it was falling out of me. I'd *never* had this reaction before. Mind you, I'd never really acted like this before. I looked at the side of Mama's face, hoping, beseeching her to look at me. She didn't.

'Go to bed, Magda,' was all I got. Again, no eye contact.

I glanced across and saw Dziadek's untouched food still on its tray. My knees felt like they were locked and my feet seemed to weigh a ton as I pushed myself towards my bedroom. What a mess! I balled up both fists and rubbed them into my eyes and, for the first time in my life, I hoped I wouldn't wake up the next morning.

Chapter eleven

Mrs Walsh, our school principal, and the rest of the senior management team filed onto the stage of the assembly hall and took their seats, ready for the annual celebration to commemorate Belview College's opening. Rows of green blazers sat in front of me, one or two Belview Babes whispering or giggling, but mostly there were straight backs and silence. We had to sit in alphabetical order in form class groups at assembly, so Sophie was only two seats away from me, all tear-stained and forlorn. Again. Mia Campbell and another girl were in front of me, whispering, their heads angled into each other.

Mrs Walsh waited for complete silence before

heading to the rostrum and talking about today as an 'auspicious occasion'.

'One hundred and ten years ago the first Belview girls walked through that door,' she said, solemnly, pointing through a window at the main entrance. 'Since then, thousands of young women have pounded these corridors and been enriched with an education that is of the finest standard in Belfast.'

I thought of Mr Benson's French class and questioned her judgement. We were barely past *Parlez-vous Francais?*

'And today we celebrate all those young ladies and all those years by displaying the talent that Belview is renowned for,' she went on, nodding her head at the audience. 'We will begin with our junior school choir!' She stretched out an arm to the thirty or so girls standing beneath the stage and facing the rest of us, every one of them earnest and ready.

The Head of Music pinged on his piano and the girls were off, singing to the heavens, with their faces changing shape according to the pitch of their notes, their mouths wide open and exaggerated. I don't know why, but it always made me want to giggle, the way their faces contorted like that. Their voices rose and fell and, with every note they hit, another butterfly attacked my stomach.

I had no idea where I was supposed to be on this

programme of talent. I just sat there, beginning to dread my turn. I looked around – I was surrounded by rich girls, girls who lived in big houses, girls who knew each other from primary schools, girls who expected and *demanded* the best that life could give them. The collar of my shirt felt too tight all of a sudden. The assembly hall was too warm. Stingy Mrs Walsh must have allowed the heat to be finally switched on.

There was a polite round of applause and then 8B's choral speaking was announced. After a few coughs and shuffles *The Rime of the Ancient Mariner* began. I silently voiced most of the words along with the Year 8s, having learnt it off by heart in my last year of primary school. I was supposed to recite it at our leavers' assembly back then, but I'd chickened out. My P7 teacher had said that he'd expected that. After 8B there was a comedy sketch, some Irish dancing and a string quartet.

And then: 'Now Magda Jankowska will read a short story from her collection.'

Shit! I looked around again at the closed windows and wondered why no-one had had the wit to open them. My shirt collar was starting to feel like a noose. I could hear whispering around me, could see senior prefects lined round the hall like guards. Girls beside me were clapping their hands as I climbed out of my row, trying not to stumble. My hair was falling around me, curtaining my face.

I climbed the steps to the stage and felt a cold sweat wash over me. Shakily, I placed my pages on the rostrum and wished my legs would settle themselves. I could hear occasional coughs, but nothing else. Just stony silence. I cleared my throat and began reading. Quietly, nervously. I could hear Mrs Walsh telling me to speak up. The vice principal came over and moved the microphone closer to me. I read out the title of my story again and reread the first paragraph. I could sense girls shuffling in their seats. I glanced up and saw Mia Campbell giggling into someone's ear. My eyes darted towards Sophie and her face was lit up, her eyes gleaming with encouragement. I rambled on, telling my story about a mystical horse that no-one could see except my granddad, a moonlight-white pony called Cloudy Bay. Mentioning my granddad's name gave me a little more confidence. I looked down again and saw Mia had stopped giggling. Sophie seemed to be really listening and Anna was sitting at the end of a row with her lips slightly parted. All the others seemed to be listening too. I read on, and on, until my voice was stronger and surer. I flipped over my page and read the next one. And the next one. And by the time I came to the end my legs were still and my voice was steady. I read the final line and there was a round of applause. Nothing outstanding, just clapping – but it wasn't tainted by sniggering or coy looks. Just clapping and eyes looking straight at me. No poison in them.

And when I took my seat and 10C started singing 'Happy', I decided that I kind of *was* happy. I had survived my most embarrassing experience at Belview College and I could hear myself quietly singing along: *Clap along if you feel like happiness is the truth.* I would survive another day at Belview College.

I felt a hand press on mine and when I looked up Sophie was reaching over to me.

'That was amazing, Maggie!'

'Thank you,' I answered. 'And sorry. Again.'

She nodded her head, closing her eyes like some sort of guru, and pulled back into her seat. I started to feel my breath come back to me, slowly, like it was unsure of itself. Melissa Jennings who was sitting next to me gave me a nudge with her elbow and a smile out of the side of her face. My heartbeat was slowing down to a steady pace and I let myself sigh – a deep sigh of relief. I had done it. I had put my head over the parapet and lived to tell the tale. I was pretty sure I could handle anything after this.

I was wrong.

'Mystical horses, Egyptian princesses – always knew you lived in Cloud Cuckoo Land,' Mia sniggered when I walked into the canteen two hours later. Chloe McKeever giggled back. Their two high ponytails swishing in unison.

I took my tray and walked on past, finding a spot at the end of a table as far away from them as possible. Anna came and joined me.

'That was good,' she said, barely audibly, and proceeded to eat her panini without any more discussion.

The canteen was loud with chatter and the clanging of plates and trays, but I could still hear Mia and the Morons yapping on about Takabuti and glancing in my direction. How did they know about my Takabuti stories?

I saw Sophie amble in, swishing her hair dramatically and queueing up sweetly at the hot food area. She cast her eyes around the hall, found mine and smiled.

After she'd got her food, she stopped to chat to Mia and her gang before heading over in my direction.

'Aw, no seats here!' she moaned. 'I'll have to sit with Mia, but we'll chat later – 'kay?'

I nodded. This girl really confused me.

'See you in Art tomorrow!' she sang out, sashaying backwards across the canteen.

I looked down at my soda-bread pizza slice and decided I wasn't hungry. The lyrics from 'Happy' were still buzzing through my head – *Clap along if you feel like a room without a roof.* That's exactly how I felt, like I was exposed. Like everyone could look down and in on me and I couldn't hide my secrets.

For the next half hour Sophie giggled along with Mia and her mates, her eyes darting towards me every now and again. At one point Mia snorted with laughter all over her panini and I'm *sure* Chloe McKeever was smirking in my direction. What the hell had Sophie told them?

'What do you think, Maggie?' Sophie asked me the next day, showing me her Hearst Castle replica. 'Do you think it's starting to resemble the photo?'

'Jeez!' I nodded.

She had built a Spanish-type castle – baroque, she called it – to resemble the home of some Californian trillionaire called William Randolph Hearst. Apparently Sophie, her mum and dad had toured California a few years back and they had stopped at this humongous home.

'That's the Casa Grande finished,' she said. 'The centrepiece of the castle.'

'Bloody hell, Sophie – there's so much detail! You must have worked on this at home.' I felt confused.

Only last week it was barely started.

'Shush, don't let on to the others – Miss Price let me take it home,' she said smugly. 'I've spent hours on those towers. Nicola thinks it's a masterpiece!'

It was. The attention to detail was awesome. I'd never seen anything like this produced by a student in our school before.

'When I set out to do something, I don't give up,' she said, painting the tiniest specks of gold on the gated entrance, her eyes narrowed in utmost concentration. 'I keep on going until I get exactly what I want,' she murmured, eyeing the model closely.

I looked at my own piece made from newspaper and card and lollipop sticks. It was supposed to be modelled on the wooden lodge my grandfather had grown up in in Masuria: basic, with a steep roof and two windows at front and back and one in the gable. Of course, I had only one wall done at this stage, so it just looked like a row of lollipop sticks painted chocolate brown – which it was. Sophie had angled and measured and used foam board and doll-house siding. She had folded paper into origami shapes to make features like window frames and balsa wood for doors.

'Sophie, this is absolutely amazing!' Miss Price called out, two hands in the air. 'My goodness,

Sophie – I've never seen anything like it in the junior school!' She clapped her hands together and then hugged Sophie like she had finally found her child-genius. Her long, red hair was hanging loose today like an untamed mane.

'*Girls, girls – come and look!*' she shouted.

The rest of our Art class climbed off their stools and came over to *ooh* and *aah* – it really was a cool piece of work! Sophie's face was lit up.

'It's brilliant, Sophie!' I said.

She hugged me and thanked me and, for the umpteenth time, she confused me.

'It's nice, isn't it?' she asked when the rest had clattered back to their desks.

'What is?'

'The glow – the feeling that you get when you're praised.'

'Yeah,' I answered, not really sure of the *glow*.

'You must have felt like that when you read your story yesterday,' she went on. 'That's why I nominated you. I knew you'd never volunteer yourself, and I *so* wanted you to get the attention you deserve.'

I cast my eyes down, unsure how to react. 'But you should have asked first, Sophie.'

'No way – then you'd have said no, you goof!' she laughed.

111

'But you know I'm not like that. I don't want to be on show. And you seem to keep – I don't know – putting the spotlight on me,' I tried to explain.

'I'm trying to bring you out of yourself, silly,' she giggled.

'But that's not your job, Sophie! You're not in charge of *bringing me out of myself*. I'm quite happy where I am!'

Her look penetrated me then. There could have been scorch marks on the wall behind me the way her eyes seemed to go right through me and out the other side. Then she beamed at me and squeezed my arm.

'OK, OK, Miss Maggie J, I get the message. You go on hiding your light under a bushel then, or whatever that saying is.' She shook her head like I was a naughty toddler. 'There'll be no more *bigging-up* coming from me.'

'Is that why you told Mia about my Takabuti story?' I asked tentatively. 'To big me up?'

There was a split-second pause. 'Yeah, that's right. I wanted those girls to know how creative and imaginative you are,' she nodded. 'I thought they might start to admire you – like I do.'

'But they don't and they won't, Sophie. They'll just keep using stuff like that to taunt me, can't you see that?'

'God, Maggie – you're so paranoid! What, is *everything* about Magda Jankowska off limits? Am I not allowed to mention you in *any* conversation? I was just trying to support you!' Her eyes flashed something – anger maybe.

I decided to drop it. Maybe I was being paranoid – or worse, maybe I was jealous of Sophie? I didn't think so, but I seemed to be the only one getting her 'wrong'. We carried on with our projects until the 3.30 bell rang out and then barely spoke as we pushed through the corridors to the lockers.

Sophie walked straight over to Mia and her cronies who were gaping out the window at something. My stomach lurched when I saw what they were looking at – or rather, *who* they were looking at.

Toni was bent over an electric leaf-blower, wearing earmuffs and singing away to himself. His jeans were riding low, showing the crack of his hairy backside. The sniggering from the girls turned into howls of laughter as a slime of sickness started to fill up my throat. Mia was pointing right at the crevice between Toni's bum cheeks. I didn't even bother getting my coat out of my locker – I turned and ran as fast as I could back down the corridor and out another door. I noticed there was no sign of Sophie behind me. Where was her support now?

Chapter twelve

When Toni arrived home, he didn't seem too bothered by girls laughing at his bum crack. Anyway, he probably hadn't seen them. He did say that he had been chatting to Sophie at the end of the day though.

'Sophie said you'd disappeared home before she got the chance to say goodbye,' he mumbled, crunching on one of Mama's cookies.

Yeah, right. She didn't get the chance because she was too busy taking the piss out of *you*, I thought to myself.

'She asked me for a lift home, but I said I couldn't,' he went on. 'Told her I wouldn't be finished for another two hours so she'd have a long wait.'

'She asked for *what?* Toni, no way! *Don't ever give lifts home to the girls from school!*' I yelled.

'Why not? I gave her a lift home on your birthday,' he answered, untying the laces of his boots.

'Toni, you mor–!' I stopped myself. 'Toni, that was different – she was a guest in our house and, anyway, Tata went with you. *You do not give lifts to schoolgirls, Toni! Got it?* She's thirteen, for God's sake!'

He was looking at me like I was the one who had lost the plot and not him. Sitting on the sofa, boots off now, looking at me like I was some kind of demon.

'What the hell does that mean?' he asked.

'You know what it means. Toni, Sophie is … well, she can be a bit sly. Just be careful.'

'You are so hard on that girl, Magda. You've got her all wrong! Some of those rich girls – she told me they were laughing at me today. I don't know why and I don't care.' He shrugged. 'But Sophie told them to get lost. She's not like them.'

So that's why she hadn't chased after me. But I was sure I'd caught her smirking along with the others, not guffawing maybe, but she was too clever for that.

I changed the subject when Mama and Tata came

116

down from Dziadek's room. They still hadn't had their *talk* with me and I knew I was still in the doghouse. But they didn't seem in the mood for a talk. Mama sat down without even mentioning what was for tea and put her head into her hands. Tata stroked her back and told her everything would be alright.

'What's wrong?' Toni asked.

'Papa,' my mum breathed. 'He is getting weaker and weaker every day. He hasn't eaten in three days. I don't know what to do.'

'We take him to the doctor's,' Toni said matter-of-factly. 'We're tax payers here, we're registered with a surgery. We get him medical help.'

Mama shook her head. 'He won't go to the doctor,' she said, her voice raspy with tiredness. 'He says he will only leave the flat if he is going home. To Poland.'

Tata threw his head up as if to say *that* was never going to happen.

'Then we *bring* the doctor to *him*,' Toni announced, standing up, resolute. 'I will phone the what-do-you-call-it – Out of Hours. I will make someone come.'

And he did. He lifted the phone and spoke in steady, stern English and insisted that they send a doctor out. He told them it would be cheaper than paying for an ambulance, which is what he was prepared to do if they didn't oblige. (He didn't tell them that there was actually no way that Dziadek would get into the ambulance!) The NHS was on its knees, or so everyone around here said, but Toni convinced them to send a locum out to see his grandfather – and he wasn't taking no for an answer. Over three hours later a young doctor arrived and went brusquely to Dziadek's room. He told the rest of us to wait.

The four of us stood there staring at each other, saying nothing. The silence hung over us like one of my *babcia*'s old quilts. I could hear Belfast going about its business outside, horns hooting, an occasional siren screaming, a dog barking. I had words inside me, but I couldn't pull them up through my throat.

The doctor finally came back down the stairs and asked to speak to Mama and Tata.

'Come on, sister, we will wait outside,' Toni said, putting his arm around my shoulders and leading me down to the door. 'We won't go far,' he said reassuringly.

The streets were covered in damp leaves and more rain clouds loomed above our heads. 'Come on, let's go in here.' Toni ushered me into a coffee shop and ordered a hot chocolate for me with marshmallows and cream on top.

The girl who served us spoke in broken English, making me look up. Toni was chatting away to her like he already knew her.

'The doctor will tell us what we need to know,' he said to me, sitting down on a leather sofa beside me. 'Then we will have to make decisions.'

'What sort of decisions?'

'About how to make him better – or how to accept that he will not be better.' He was nodding his head, as if he was processing all this in his own brain. 'We will have to be brave, Magda. OK?'

'OK.'

My big brother could be so sensible sometimes. Right now I was glad of his stocky arm around my shoulders, and even though he smelt faintly of sweat and soil, I huddled into him. We sat like that for a while, hoping and waiting.

The waitress came over and asked if we wanted anything else. She gave Toni a wide-beamed smile and he was all chat back to her with his 'No, thank you's' and small talk.

'Who is she?' I asked him when she went back behind the counter.

'Modesta,' he answered, speaking the name like it was precious silk. 'Isn't it a beautiful name?'

'Suppose. Where's she from?'

'Lithuania. She has been in Belfast for three years.'

He was still smiling at her, watching her while she frothed up a latte.

'She says she is applying for a passport here,' he went on. 'But cannot decide which is better – Irish or British. Lithuania does not allow her to have more than one passport, though, so she will have to give her Lithuanian one up. And she's not completely sure she wants to do that.'

I rolled my eyes, thinking how bloody mixed up the world was, especially here in Ulster. In Belfast you could be Irish, or British, or even narrow it down to Northern Irish. And that's before you mixed in Polish or Lithuanian or Bangladeshi or whatever. No bloody wonder people didn't know what to call themselves. No wonder *I* didn't know what to call myself. Did you belong to the country you lived in? Or the country you came from? What the heck was I – *Br-Irish*, Polish, or just me?

'Come on, we will go back now.' Toni set a new pound coin on the counter and told Modesta he would see her the next day, making me wonder how well he actually *did* know her. I noticed they spoke to each other in Polish.

'Her mother was Polish,' Toni explained as if sensing my question.

We kicked at the leaves on our way back, my stomach in knots at the thought of what Mama and

Tata were going to tell us. Out of the corner of my eye I spotted a hoody hovering. It was Colin, arms folded, looking like he was waiting for something. He spotted me and Toni and turned and walked away.

'He said that he can't be sure of Papa's diagnosis until he goes into hospital for tests,' Mama said, her arms folded around her stomach like she was in pain.

'But he won't go to hospital,' Toni replied, stating the obvious.

'We know that,' Tata said. 'But we are going to have to find a way to convince him.' He was sitting beside Mama on the sofa, rubbing her back, trying to soothe her but she kept rocking back and forwards. 'The doctor said his pulse is very slow and he is weak through not eating. He suspects other things too but he cannot say without referring him for tests.'

'Can I go see him?' I asked, still standing like a spectre in the doorway. Mama and Tata nodded.

Dziadek was in bed when I went into his room. There was a glass of water and some tablets on his bedside table. His eyes were closed but I crept towards him anyway. Looking down on him, remembering all the years we'd had together, I felt like I was choking. He used to make me giggle when he used to say that he was born ancient. 'I had old man's glasses and wrinkles when I was in my cot, Magda,' he used to say. He used to have his shirtsleeves rolled up to the elbow back in Poland, searching through the soil with his hands like he was reading Braille. I used to cling to the edge of his trousers and watch him, my knees pointed and muddy.

'Magda,' he said quietly, opening his eyes. 'Where have you been?'

I realised I hadn't seen him since yesterday morning.

'At school, outside, out and about, Dziadek,' I answered, omitting one or two temper tantrums and hooking up with a hungry hoody called Colin.

He took my hand and I shuddered at how cold it felt. The room was well-heated, but his skin was like touching cold porridge.

'The doctor says I must go to hospital for tests, Magda. I will not go to hospital, child. I will only go home.' Tears were streaking his cheeks and I could see the tiredness in his face.

'When you are better we will take you home for a visit, Dziadek. But first we have to make you better – and the people in the hospital know how to do that.'

'Magda, Magda,' he said weakly, shaking his head, 'I will not be made better. I want to leave soon. Please, please, tell this to Katarina. Please!'

The lines around his eyes were like cracks in plaster, his voice as feeble as I'd ever heard it.

'Now, go please. I need to sleep. But come back in the morning before you go to school. I like to see you before you go to lessons.'

'OK,' I answered, adding 'I love you, Dziadek,' before I left the room.

Chapter thirteen

November gales shook us all through a month of Dziadek's decline, as he sank lower and lower every day and refused to go to hospital. Drains gurgled at me and traffic splashed me on my way to school each day, and then just as fiercely the frost set in. Sophie and I had carried on with some sort of uneasy alliance: her as gushing as ever and me suspecting everything she said and did. Even Anna seemed tired of my suspicion.

Then one Friday morning, as I slipped and slid over the unsalted road outside school, Sophie skidded past in a silver Mercedes. Her mum drove a red car so I knew it wasn't Nicola dropping her off. She gave me an exaggerated wave as the car turned into Belview College's avenue, nearly mowing down a few Belview Babes in the process. The car passed me again on the way out, taking no prisoners as it spun back onto the main road.

'That was my dad!' Sophie yelped at me as soon as I stepped inside the foyer. 'He's home for Christmas!'

Christmas was still three weeks away but I was glad for her. Genuinely glad.

'That's great, Sophie!' I said, thinking about how weird it would be not to see my own dad for six months.

'*And* he's staying with us!' she added, crossing her fingers. 'Who knows? Maybe the Ice Queen's heart is melting?'

I wasn't sure who had left who: Nicola or Ben. Sophie had said that her mum had missed Ireland and insisted on coming back, but then why was she talking about Nicola as an Ice Queen? And, as far as I could tell, her mum and dad still went on holiday together.

'We're going to have a proper family Christmas. Just like your family,' she beamed, taking me as usual by the arm.

I hadn't really thought about ours as a 'proper' family Christmas – it certainly wasn't traditional Christmas dinner in a Belfast sense. But I decided

126

against correcting her and let her babble on. Her dad was buying her a new iPhone for Christmas, she said, and taking her clothes-shopping and splashing out on a Spa day at the Culloden Hotel for her and her mum. I had asked for the new Katie Perry album and the latest book from my favourite author and I knew I'd be lucky – and happy – to get those.

Mia Campbell swung her ponytail in my face as she walked past with Chloe, calling out a 'Hey, chick!' to Sophie and totally ignoring me. Sophie didn't seem to notice. She was still talking about the *epic* Christmas she was going to have.

We headed into our form room where Mr Mawhinney was already logged on to his computer. When he'd first arrived with us, he'd changed all the seating around so that I was seated in the second row in the middle with a girl called Emma. Sophie had begged him to let her swap with Emma and, faced with Sophie's pleading face, he'd given in. Now I think he was beginning to regret it because Sophie never stopped rabbiting on to me.

He started to call out the register from SIMS: Emma Atwood, Jenny Browne, Charlotte Caldwell … By the time he got to me I was knee-deep in Sophie's tales of 'Ben's going to do this and Ben's going to do that'.

'Magda?' he called again.

'Oh, sorry, sir. Yes – present.'

'In body at least,' he said, smiling. 'Oh, by the way, Magda, I wanted to talk to you about the Christmas concert. Will you stay behind for a moment after registration?'

'Erm, yes, sir,' I answered, thinking what the heck?

Sophie elbowed me and gave me a wink and said something stupid like 'Get in, girl!'

When the rest piled out of the room, Mr Mawhinney went on pressing keys on his keyboard. Belview College had *the* most up-to-date computers and software, which was weirdly inconsistent with the ancient dark-wooded desks and floors all around us. I stood looking at the bare skeleton of the oak trees outside, ghostly-looking in this morning's frost while Mr M was still tap-tapping away. I cast my eyes towards the clock on the wall behind him, thinking I was going to get into trouble with *Monsieur* Benson if he didn't get a move on.

'Ah, sorry, Magda. Just needed to send that report through to Mrs Walsh. Now,' he said, 'the Christmas concert.'

'I don't sing, sir, or play an instrument,' I said, changing my weight onto my left foot.

'No, that's fine. This year's event will be more of a variety performance – recitals, short plays, as well

128

as music. Mrs Walsh has asked me to help organise it, so I thought I would *mix it up* a bit,' he said, emphasising the 'mix it up' like he was a dude *down with the kids*.

I could see where this was going.

'I heard your story at the anniversary event back in October. I thought it was wonderful. Perhaps you might read another one for us at Christmas?'

Oh God, not again. I could almost hear myself groaning inwardly.

'I know – I know what you're going to say, Magda. That you're not into that kind of thing and I get that. Really, I do. I used to want to hide out below the radar too.' He smiled. 'But it's good to challenge yourself. And you've got talent – you should display it.'

He beckoned his Year 10 class in and told me to think about it.

'Don't say no *straight* away,' he laughed as I made my way out. 'We'll talk again tomorrow.'

I threw my bag over my shoulder and made my way towards the languages corridor. Stopping on the landing after the first flight of stairs, I spied my dad through the window. He was throwing rock salt down on the netball court, making sure that the Belvies wouldn't slip and hurt themselves at break and lunchtime. Some of them threw a few shots in between classes, but most of them just paraded around in groups, taking the air like a bunch of society ladies in a Jane Austen novel.

I watched Tata for a few moments, hunched over, heavy-coated. I couldn't help thinking that he should be *inside*, teaching. Not sifting coarse grit through his cold, calloused hands, his breath coming out in little clouds. I felt sort of heavy as I watched him, like the stones in my coat pockets. Then I caught sight of Toni, over by the bird feeders at the corner of the hockey pitch. Frost crusted the grass, the kind of frost that would hold your footprints for days. There'd be no hockey or camogie played on that pitch today, I was thinking, as I watched the birds come to Toni, pecking at nuts and seeds.

'Magda? Why aren't you in class?'

Mrs Walsh had stepped up behind me without me noticing.

'Erm, sorry, Mrs Walsh – I – I'm on my way now,' I blustered.

She looked out the window and saw my father and brother.

'Your family works hard,' she said, nodding her head and watching them. 'As do you, Magda. Your grades have always been very good. But don't let standards slip, Magda. Off you go before you miss any more class. Where should you be?'

'French, Mrs Walsh.'

'Then get going. *Au revoir*,' she said, lifting her hand in the direction of the languages rooms.

I scurried off, the school echoing around me with the sound of silent corridors. I mumbled an excuse to Mr Benson and sat down at my desk. Luckily my seat in French was right beside the radiator.

'*Merci, Mademoiselle Magda*. So good of you to grace us with your presence,' Mr Benson said, turning back to the white board to conjugate the verb *to catch*. He chanted through *J'ai attraper, vous attrapez, il attrape* ... while I scribbled it all quickly down in my exercise book.

'What did Mr Mawhinney want?' Sophie whispered from the desk behind.

'He wants me to read another one of my stories.'

'When?'

'At the Christmas concert. Well, it's not just a concert this year. It ...'

'Magda Jankowska, now that you're actually *in* the classroom would it be too much to ask that you concentrate on what *I'm* saying and not Miss Long behind you?' Mr Benson barked.

'Sorry, sir,' I answered, wondering how many times I was going to end up apologising to teachers before this day was over. I'd managed three already and it wasn't even 9.30!

Sophie wasn't going to be put off though. She slipped me a note, but I pushed it under my pencil case, deciding it could wait until the 10 o'clock bell.

As soon as we were out of the classroom she was beside me.

'I don't think you should do it, Maggie. The story, I mean.'

'You've changed your tune.'

'I know. But I thought about what you said, about it not being my job to big you up and bring you out of yourself and stuff. You were right. And you were right about not letting people force you to do things. Mr Mawhinney shouldn't be putting pressure on you. Nobody should.' She flicked her glossy hair as if that ended the lecture.

'Where has all this come from?' I asked. 'What happened to all that guff about me hiding my light under a bushel?'

'I was wrong. Hide your light. Be yourself. Don't let anybody change you,' she said, all earnest eyes. 'God, I got you so wrong, didn't I, Maggie? But now I get it – just let Maggie be Maggie. That's what my dad said anyway.' She gave her mane another flick.

'You were talking to your dad about this?'

'Yeah, he's like a guru,' she said, all American-accented all of a sudden. 'He said people should never change.'

She nodded her head in what I'm sure she thought was a wise way, but internally I was questioning how prudent her dad's words were. I was glad that she was going to stop pushing me into things, but this abrupt U-turn had me flummoxed. And I was even more flummoxed in Miss Patterson's English class when Sophie advised me to pretend I'd forgotten to do my homework.

'You hate drawing attention to yourself, so just be like everybody else and say you'll bring it in tomorrow.'

'But that's dumb,' I said. 'I've got my essay right here.'

'But *Maaggie!*' she said, drawing my name out like I was a moron. 'Your essay will be better than everyone else's and Mrs P will start heaping praise on you and the other girls will hate you for being so bloody brilliant at everything. Just be like us,' she added perkily.

Now this had me totally confused. I *was* always saying that I didn't want to stand out, that I didn't want to make myself a target. My mid-term grades back at Halloween were embarrassingly high and teachers were actually starting to notice me. And Mia and the Morons were jealous as hell. Maybe Sophie had a point.

She winked at me like some wise old Aunt Sally

and went to her desk beside Chloe McKeever.

So when Mrs Patterson asked for the essays on Lady Macbeth, I didn't hand mine up. And both Sophie and Chloe gave me a big thumbs-up.

Chapter fourteen

'Come and say hello to Ben!'

Sophie grabbed my hand at the lockers and pulled me outside to her dad's silver Mercedes after the 3 o'clock bell. 'Ben' had pulled into a space reserved for Mrs Walsh who had obviously left the building.

'Hello, Mr Long,' I said.

'Call me Ben, honey,' he said, like something out of an American sit-com. 'You want a lift home?'

'Erm, no – it's fine. I'll get the bus, Mr … Ben.'

'Mr Ben!' Sophie screeched. 'That's your new name, Dad,' she laughed. 'Hey, Mags, there's *your* dad – why don't we introduce our padres?'

Tata was painting a wooden fence by the front

entrance, lost in concentration as always. Sophie ran over to him and obviously talked him into taking a short break because he put his brush down and came towards us.

I went to meet him. He was smelling of Cuprinol and wearing his brightest smile.

'Hello, love. Had a good day at school?' he said in Polish.

'Yes, Tata.'

'I won't give you a hug because I'm covered in varnish. And anyway, I know it's not *allowed*.' He grinned, referring to my rule of him and Toni keeping out of my way at school.

We reached Ben and Tata switched to English. 'Please to meet you, Mr Long,' he said. 'I'll not shake your hand for reasons that are obvious.' He smiled, showing his stained, wet hand.

'Pleased to meet you too, Mr –?'

'Jankowski.'

I couldn't help noticing that my dad knew Sophie's father's surname, but Ben didn't know my father's. He was friendly enough though, not gushing like Sophie, but chatty. He complained about the cold weather and the unsalted roads and how it was thirty degrees when he left Thailand.

'I can't imagine thirty degrees at this time of year,' Tata said. 'Back in Poland it's even colder than here.'

'Speaking of cold, I'm freezing standing here,' Sophie interrupted. 'Mr Jankowski, can Maggie come back to our house for a little while? We'll drop her home in time for dinner, won't we, Ben?'

'I have no objections,' my dad said. 'That's OK with me. OK with you, Magda?'

It was only sort of OK, but I was kind of stuck, so I said yes.

'See you later, Tata. Will you phone Mama and tell her where I am?'

'Seriously, Mags – you need to get your own phone!' Sophie laughed, climbing into the front passenger seat of her dad's car. If she only knew that my dad had only recently bought himself a mobile phone so getting one for me was way down our list of priorities!

Mr Long sped out of the school's avenue like he was in a slalom race and within minutes we were at number 185 Chester Road.

'Come on, I'll make us a snack,' Sophie offered.

I followed her down the hallway and into the shiny kitchen at the back. The inside of the house was like an oven. Clearly no worries about heating bills in this house.

'Fancy a pancake? I made them last night when Nicola and Ben were out. *Instead* of doing my English homework,' she giggled. 'Oh, and this is my blackberry jam. I made this back in the autumn.'

'*Wow!*' I said. 'Clever you. Is there anything you can't make? Pancakes, jams, castles!' I laughed. 'You're a one-woman creation station!'

'My daughter is *very* skilled,' Ben said, putting an arm around her. 'But, unfortunately, her grades at Belview do not reflect that. She should *not* be neglecting homework in favour of pancakes. We might have to consider moving schools again, pumpkin.' He said this with a tight smile, one that made Sophie's face crumple like a tissue.

'*Dad!* Not again!'

'I'm going to have a chat with your mum about it,' he said, lifting his arm away. 'You two eat.'

Sophie growled under her breath as he left, muttering something about chatting turning into screaming.

'You OK?' I asked.

'*Duuhh*, no!'

'He won't really take you out of Belview, will he?'

'*Yeeess!* He will. He doesn't want a pancake-maker, he wants a doctor! Or a lawyer! *Always. Bloody. Has!*' She spat out the words as she banged a plate down in front of me. 'Jam?' she asked, holding up a knife.

'Yeah, I think I'd better,' trying to make a joke about the floating knife.

'And the joke is, he runs a flippin' B&B!' she said, plunging the knife into the blackberry jam. 'And *she* colours in and buys paintings for a living! How come they get to be creative but I have to be practical!'

The knife was still waving and pointing.

'Can you really see me giving a toss about someone's bowel movements?' she hissed.

'Erm, not really,' I said. Unhelpfully.

I had never heard Sophie talk like this about her parents before. She always seemed to idolise them. Her eyes flinted like the steel-grey surfaces in the kitchen and I wondered where her gloss had disappeared to. I could hear raised voices coming from upstairs and suddenly I didn't feel like blackberry jam.

'*Grrr!* They're at it again! They came back from the exhibition last night slamming doors and screaming at each other,' she said, her voice lower now.

And yet Sophie was all thrilled this morning at her dad being here – there'd been no sign of any angst about her parents fighting. And something else didn't add up either.

'I thought your dad said that you shouldn't try to change people – you know – turn them into something they're not,' I said, choosing my words carefully in case she blew up again.

'Oh, that was just about you,' she said with a shrug.

'What do you mean?' I asked, feeling really uncomfortable all of a sudden.

And suddenly the gloss was back in a flash. 'Oh, just that you're amazing as you are, and that I should just let you be yourself,' she said with a shiny smile, her head cocked to one side. 'Oh, look! It's Charlie!' she gasped as she glanced out through the French windows. 'Hang on a sec, Mags. I really want to see him about something.'

Funny. She'd never seemed that bothered about their gardener-cum-caretaker-cum-handyman before. I watched as she went outside and started speaking to Charlie. Whatever it was she was talking about, it looked serious. She was all arm-waving and intense, and Charlie was kind of glaring back at her and then striding off. It was like sitting in the middle of a soap opera. Except that, funnily enough, the shouting match upstairs seemed to have stopped.

'That's that sorted,' she said, coming back inside and wiping her hands as if she was cleaning them. 'Like the pancakes?'

I figured she was too volatile right at that minute, so I decided not to tell her that they were way too sweet. She must have put a bag of sugar in them.

'Hello, you two.'

Nicola appeared behind us. I hadn't even heard footsteps on the stairs. She was as neat and pretty as always, with not a hint of an argument hanging around her. She grabbed a spare pancake and *oohed* and *aahhed* about how delicious they were and then said she would run me home. I felt as if I'd only just arrived, but I wasn't about to argue. The atmosphere in this house was as thick as Sophie's jam so I nodded my head and bade my goodbyes. Boy, these people could go from hot to ice-cold and back again within a micro-second!

'Radlan Street, isn't that right?' Nicola was asking me, reversing her red Golf out of the garage.

'Yes, Mrs Long. Sorry to be a nuisance.'

'You're not a nuisance, Maggie. And don't call me Mrs Long – it makes me feel way too old,' she said with a smile. 'Sorry about the raised voices. Ben and I don't always see eye to eye about what Sophie should and shouldn't do.'

'It's fine,' I shrugged, a bit embarrassed that she'd even brought it up.

'Ben thinks it's all about grades. He went nuts when he saw her mid-term results last night.'

Again, this puzzled me. Sophie looked so happy with her dad only just this morning. The Longs obviously recovered from rows very quickly.

'Good job he lives in Thailand,' she went on, rolling her eyes.

I couldn't imagine my mum talking about my dad like this to a random teenager. Did everybody in Belfast over-share?

'He wants Sophie to go over there with him in March. Says he's found her a good school. I'm just not having it, Maggie.' She breathed out slowly, her fingers dancing on the steering wheel.

'How does Sophie feel about that?' I asked, unsure of my place in this discussion. I didn't know whether she wanted a passive listener or a real one.

'Sophie thinks Thailand is heaven,' she said, her lips curled down. 'But she's only been there for holidays. She doesn't know what her dad's really like when he's working and has no time to stop and be with her. *I* do.'

Yikes! This was getting far too personal. I was thirteen, for goodness' sake, not a marriage guidance counsellor.

'Just take a left here,' I said, hoping to change the subject.

'Oh, I know where I'm going, Maggie – this was my old stomping ground,' she said, turning the steering wheel. 'I grew up around here. On Station Avenue.'

I knew my jaw had dropped but I couldn't help it.

142

I was just so gobsmacked. Nicola with her perfect bob and expensive clothes grew up around here? Seriously? I looked at the redbrick houses with their minute back yards and boarded-up windows and I just couldn't picture Nicola Long living in one of them.

'I used to love to run down to the railway bridge and feel the whoosh and vibration of the train running underneath. I shiver when I think of the number of times I ran across those tracks, Maggie. Nobody was shouting about health and safety back then!' She laughed.

I was still looking at her like she had two heads. She started really laughing then, a brittle, cawing sound.

'You're shocked, aren't you, Maggie?'

'Erm, just a little,' I said.

'You should see where Ben came from then!' She laughed again. 'Is this yours here? Above the shop?' she asked, pulling in outside Michal's. 'You want me to see you in?'

'It's OK, Mrs ... I mean, Nicola. Thanks very much for the lift.'

I got out. The air was crisping up again and I could feel a cold breeze blow into my mouth. Nicola reversed and turned and sped out of Radlan Street like she was glad to get away from it. I felt a motion behind my back and whipped round to see a grey hoody.

'What – is it time for *Game of Stones* again?' I asked.

The hood came down. It was Colin.

'I don't play that game any more,' he smirked. 'Wanna go round to the park?'

'Nah, I haven't even set foot inside yet. I've been at a friend's house. I think.'

'You *think* you were at her house?'

'I *know* I was at her house – I'm just not sure if she's a friend. A true friend.'

'Way too deep for me,' he shrugged. 'So, no to the park?'

'No to the park. But why don't you come inside with me. You look frozen.'

He scraped his foot backwards and forwards on the tarmac and shrugged his shoulders again. I took that for a yes.

'Come on, then.'

He came and in we went.

'Hi, Michal. Been busy today?' I asked, walking into the shop.

'Busy every day, Magda. It seems everyone in Belfast wants to try our *pierogi*. Your mama makes them just right.'

Most of the stuff in Michal's shop was prepacked

and imported from Poland, but he had a fresh deli area that Mama worked in and her dumplings, soups and stews were becoming really popular.

'I have customers coming from Bangor for your mother's soups and dumplings,' Michal said proudly. 'Katarina keeps me in business!' He laughed – a big, beefy laugh, just like himself. Michal was from Krakow and had grown up knowing his family's tragic history. His father was Jewish and had died in a way that no-one could bring themselves to describe. That probably accounted for Michal's love of life and love of everyone around him. He had been so good to us, letting my mum work hours that suited us and renting the flat to us at a rock-bottom price. He was good with Dziadek too, chatting to him in his own language and talking about things that mattered to him.

'Who is your friend?'

'This is Colin. He lives nearby.'

'Hello, Colin. You need a job?'

Colin's head reeled back in surprise.

'I mean part-time, of course,' Michal explained. 'Just a bit of lifting and carrying.'

This was typical of Michal – he just came right out with things. No beating around the bush.

'Erm, yeah,' was all Colin could manage. 'Like, when?'

'Some evenings, Saturdays,' Michal said. 'But I have to trust you. Are you honest?' He came right over to Colin, looking him square in the eyes.

'Am I?' Colin turned to me.

'You're asking me?' I laughed. 'Colin, I barely know you.'

'Yeah, but … well, you give me the time of day, so I must be alright, mustn't I?'

Realising he needed assurance, I nodded my head.

'Michal, why don't you take Colin on for a trial period? Until, say, after Christmas? Then both of you have a get-out clause if you need one.'

'Good thinking, Magda,' Michal said, tapping his forehead. 'You've got it all going on up here. Brains to burn!' And he turned to a steaming pot of dumplings, calling out to Colin over his shoulder to turn up the next day

Colin followed me up the narrow stairs and into the flat, his hands dug deep in his pockets and his shoulders hunched. He was the complete opposite of Sophie. When she first entered our home she literally swanned in like a princess. Colin would hardly meet anyone's eye. I introduced him to Mama and he looked like a rabbit caught in the headlights.

'You would like stay for tea, Colin?' she asked in her broken English.

Colin just shrugged his shoulders which I took to be a yes.

'Do you need to let your parents know?' I asked him.

This time he just shook his head. A man of few words – *definitely* the opposite of Sophie!

I noticed Mama eying him curiously, probably wondering where his manners were or where I'd dragged him in from. But, somehow, I knew that Colin was harmless and his 'bad' manners were just nerves, awkwardness.

I took him up the stairs to meet Dziadek and was surprised to find him sitting up in bed. In recent weeks he'd been mostly sleeping.

'Hello, Dziadek,' I said, taking his hand and sitting on the side of his bed. 'This is Colin. He lives … nearby.' Truth was, I didn't know where exactly Colin lived.

'When is Christmas, Magda?' he asked, staring intently into my face. He didn't seem to even see Colin.

'Just under three weeks away, Dziadek. Why?'

His head started to nod as if he was concentrating on something, his lips moving as if he was counting.

'Then in one month it is New Year?' he asked.

'That's right,' I nodded.

Dziadek's face broke into a smile. His eyes were

less glassy than they had been in months. 'Good, good,' he said, patting my hand. 'Very good.'

I was used to Dziadek confusing me in recent months so I didn't ask why he was looking forward to the New Year. Truth was, I was *afraid* to ask. I pulled the pale-blue quilt up round him and kissed him on the forehead. His head was already back down on the pillow and his eyes closing over. The room was starting to smell musty from weeks of bed rest and was feeling less and less like our little den.

When I turned round to Colin, he was standing over by the little arched window, staring out into the Belfast evening sky. Row upon row of red-bricked houses reached all the way up to the Belfast mountains.

'Can you see your home from here?' I asked, joining him at the window.

'No,' he said, barely audible. 'But I can see the house that I live in.'

I wasn't quite sure what to say to that. I looked around the room again. Our flat was threadbare and basic, but it *was* home, no matter how much I tried to deny it. Sophie's mansion was pure luxury, but would it be really her *home* for much longer if her dad was taking her away to Thailand?

I glanced again at Dziadek and saw that he was smiling in his sleep, probably the only one of us truly at home – even if it was in his dreams.

Chapter fifteen

'So, Magda, you're on next.'

Mr Mawhinney was lining us up at the side of the stage. The Christmas concert was only two days away now and we'd barely had any practice because of Winter Assessment week. The assembly hall was coming down with decorations as old as the school but there was a brand-new Christmas tree at the front entrance which was pretty impressive.

The school technician had spent the morning trying to get the sound system right for the concert, but it was still coming out in squeaks and whistles.

'Just adjust the microphone if you need to,' Mr M said to me once the sound level was a decibel lower than eardrum-splitting.

My stomach was tight with nerves, but I had already agreed to read one of my short stories and I knew I couldn't back out now. Our form teacher had been co-ordinating the whole event and I didn't want to throw him into another fluster by getting cold feet at this late stage.

I read out the opening page and then moved off, letting Emma follow up with her tin whistle solo. We were only doing short rehearsals because there were thirty acts in total and we just needed to practice our mic 'voices'.

'*Magda! Magda!*' Tata was calling me to the side of the stage in a loud whisper.

'What's wrong? You're not even supposed to be in here, Dad,' I growled back.

'It's your brother. He's had an accident. I need to go see him, but I can't find Mrs Walsh. Can you let her know?'

Tata's face was grey with shock.

'Oh my God – is he alright? Is he badly hurt?'

'I don't know, Magda. I received a call from Sophie's father saying Toni had fallen downstairs at their house. I need to go there now. I have a taxi waiting.'

'*What the heck was he doing at Sophie's house?*' I called out to his back, but Dad was already halfway down the corridor.

My insides lurched, not just at the thought of Toni being injured, but at Toni being at Sophie's house. And up the stairs. What the hell was going on? I ran back over to Mr M and explained that I needed to see the principal.

I tore up the administration corridor and knocked on her PA's door.

'Mrs Jennings, is Mrs Walsh free? I really need to see her!' I burst out.

'My goodness, Magda, it's not often we see you at the principal's office,' she said, smiling, looking at me over her glasses. 'But I'm afraid she's in a meeting right now. Do you want me to pass on a message?'

I garbled the message and turned back onto the corridor, nausea seeping up my throat. *What* was Toni doing at Sophie's house? I knew she wasn't coming to school today because her mum was taking her on a girly Christmas shopping day. Not that her dad approved of that – apparently, he'd had a 'meltdown' at her missing school for something so 'trivial'. My mind was racing, hoping that Toni hadn't done something stupid.

Carols were booming out now on the system and there was a general feeling of winding down around the school before the holidays. But my stomach was winding up – into knots.

I sat through the rest of the rehearsals, but I couldn't think straight. Mia and her Miseries were doing a Little Mix tribute act, all pouting and gyrating until Mr M told them maybe they should tone it down. Some sixth formers were doing a sort of *Riverdance* routine and then Grace Clements from Year 10 did a solo of 'Silent Night' which just hushed the whole place down. I could feel the hairs stand up on the back of my neck.

I kept checking my watch and wished to God that I had a mobile phone. This waiting for news of Toni was killing me.

'Magda Jankowska?'

Mrs Jennings was summoning me towards her at the door. 'Magda, can you come with me for a minute?'

I followed her back down the corridor and I swear I thought my stomach was hanging out of me like a cat in a bag. She was wittering away and telling me that everything was fine, but I couldn't breathe until she led me into Mrs Walsh's office.

'Magda, sit down,' she said, nodding to the chair opposite her.

Apart from my first day at Belvoir College, I had never been in this room. I was kind of shocked to see paintings and written work from students all over the walls. There were mechanisms made in Technology class and sculptures from Art, and most weirdly of all, maths' working-outs on the wall behind her.

'If you look over there, Magda, you'll see a copy of your story about Takabuti,' she smiled, pointing towards the window. 'Now, I know you'll be anxious about your brother, so I'll put you out of your misery.' She folded her hands and leaned forward on her desk. 'He has torn ligaments in his foot and hurt his shoulder somehow too. Your father is with him in Accident & Emergency at the moment – he asked me to fill you in on all of this.'

'Does Mama know?'

She nodded. 'I believe your father rang her before he rang me,' she said.

I was relieved, but I still needed to know why he was at Sophie's house.

'Do you know … do you know why Toni was at the Longs' house?' I said and coughed.

'Yes. Apparently Mr Long has some spare roof tiles in his garage which he suggested could be used to fill up the gap in the sports hall roof. Your brother was over there checking to see if they were suitable.'

The sobs came up out of my throat before I could stop them. My whole body started to shiver and tremble.

'Goodness, Magda, are you all right?' Mrs Walsh came round to my side of the desk and looked at me in utter confusion. 'Your brother is going to be alright – honestly.'

She put a hand out to touch my shoulder and then obviously thought better of it.

Mrs Jennings sailed in to save the day with a cup of hot, sweet tea and told the principal she was needed in the canteen and that she would 'sort this out'. I cried like a baby on Mrs Jennings' shoulder for about ten solid minutes, never once explaining why I was so relieved. Never once needing to, because she just sat there in silence and let me sob. Without consulting Mrs Walsh, she walked me to the bus stop and let me go home early to Mama.

I was actually surprised to find Mama behind the counter in Michal's shop. And to see Colin there too.

'Mama, are you OK? You've heard about the accident?'

'Yes, yes, my love. Everything is OK, don't worry. Toni won't be able to work for a while, but the school said his job is safe.'

I had expected her to be in a state, but she was calmer than me. I told her I'd been sent home early, so she handed me a brush and told me to sweep the floor.

'Everything is fine, Magda. Stop worrying.' Her plait swung as she turned from one oven to the other, ably assisted by Colin who was carrying bags of flour into the little kitchen area of the shop. He was as clean and tidy as I'd ever seen him, and he looked fitter too.

'Is there something your father is not telling me?' she asked, stopping mid-turn.

'No, no, Mama. I'm just being a cry-baby. I guess I just got a shock, that's all.'

I pushed a loose strand of hair behind my ear and shook away my thoughts. How on earth could I tell her that I thought Sophie had lured Toni to her house? And up the stairs to her bedroom? It sounded totally ridiculous. I felt like a prat for getting it all wrong. Again.

The door of the shop pinged every two minutes with customers and I realised I was just in the way. I stooped to take a look at the *jaselka* – the crib – that Michal had placed in the window. Baby Jesus was, of course, absent and wouldn't appear until Christmas morning. The Joseph figurine was beginning to look past its sell-by date, with one arm missing and the facial features almost worn away, but Michal's wife had brought the crib from Poland and swore that none of it would ever be replaced. I smiled to myself, my heart rate *almost* back to normal, and made my way up the stairs to see Dziadek.

He was again sitting up in bed, again asking me how many days and weeks until the New Year. My smile evaporated as I looked at his papery-thin eyelids, his yellowness, but each time he spoke of the New Year the life came back to his blue eyes.

'Thirteen more days, Magda. Thirteen more days.'

For a few moments he was teeming with life, electric even. Then, as usual, once he had the days counted, he settled back down to sleep. I watched his lips move slightly and his features move as he fell into yet another dream. He was probably back in Masuria by now. I almost envied him.

I sat in the chair by the window, looking around the room at his books and his slightly discoloured map on the wall. Masuria was right up in the North East, near Russia, and I noticed that Dziadek had pinned the city of Olsztyn which was our nearest large town and the capital of the region. I remembered how he and Babcia used to take Toni and me to Olsztyn at the start of December and ask us to choose our ideal present for the feast of St Nicholas on the sixth of December. Of course, when we were younger we used to be amazed that St Nicholas managed to leave the very same 'ideal' present that we had picked in Olsztyn.

I must have sat reminiscing and watching Granddad for over an hour before I heard the front door bang and Tata calling me.

'Magda, come and help me with your brother!'

Dad was helping Toni up the narrow stairs, but they weren't getting very far. I let Toni lean on my shoulder too as I led them up, two steps in front, until we finally got him into the flat.

Toni's forehead was wet with sweat as he fell back into a chair.

'Get him something for his foot, Magda – he has to keep it raised up,' Tata said, wrapping some ice in a cloth.

Toni grimaced as I placed his balloon of a foot on a pile of cushions.

'What the heck happened, Toni?'

'I'll tell you later,' he said, shaking his head. 'I'm tired.'

This was *so* not like Toni. My brother would usually love to make a drama out of a story like this, not turn his head away.

'Go down to Michal's and get him some hot dumplings, Magda. He needs something warm inside him to help with the shock.'

'No, Tata. I'm not hungry. Just … just leave me for a while. You need to go and pick up the car at the Longs' house. I'll just rest.'

Toni refusing food? There was something not right here.

'You want me to go with you, Tata?' I asked.

Dad nodded and we set off for Chester Road and

left Toni in peace. I wanted to see Mr Long for myself and check out this whole *tile* story. My worries were creeping back in and Toni's offhand behaviour was making me even more suspicious. But when we arrived at the house no-one answered the door.

We got back into the car and drove back, none the wiser.

Chapter sixteen

The Christmas concert came and went, and I survived it without any major nervous breakdowns. The audience clapped politely at my story and I came down from the stage relatively unscathed. Toni hadn't said anything more about the accident, despite my questions, and weirdly Sophie hadn't come back to school the following day. Her mum must have taken her on one hell of a shopping trip!

By now we were on our school holidays and it was the day before Christmas Eve. I used to *love* the 24th December back in Poland. We'd start the day by fasting, then lighting the tree lights and having an absolute feast in the evening. We would watch out for the first star to appear in the sky and that's when the feast would begin. We'd stuff ourselves with fish, usually carp, and then feel sick on Christmas morning but *still* be dragged out to church.

'Thank you for helping in the shop today, Magda. It's useful to have an extra pair of hands to serve the customers while your mama slaves away at the stove,' Michal chuckled, his thick, black moustache wriggling as he laughed. 'Colin has been a good help too. I thought he looked a bit scrawny when I first saw him, but he can lift industrial-size bags of flour like feathers!' He roared with laughter, loving his own little 'joke'.

Colin wasn't quite so scrawny any more. As it turned out, he'd been working in Michal's every single day since he'd been taken on – schooldays and all – and he was putting away more dumplings than the customers by the looks of it.

'Does your mum not mind you missing school?' I had asked him one day. His response was the obligatory shoulder-shrug.

'Colin, please carry Mrs Domanska's bags to the bus stop for her,' Michal told him now, seeing his most regular customer struggle with her *piernik* – gingerbread – ingredients of honey, lard, sugar, flour and eggs in one hand, and her large container of braised sauerkraut in the other.

'*Dziekuje* – thank you, Colin.' Mrs Domanska grinned up at him. I could see that she had grown to like him over the past few weeks.

Off they went, with her chatting away to him in Polish and him answering back in English, neither knowing what the other was saying, but not seeming to care.

The shop was steaming with warmth and spicy aromas and I noticed Mama's cheeks were as pink as the beetroots she was boiling. I could see she was enjoying herself and I was so glad, because I knew she had been worried about Dziadek. But in the past week or so she seemed to have found her peace with his illness, and with a lot of things. She seemed so, I don't know – calm. Even Toni's accident hadn't fazed her.

'You need anything, Mama?' I asked her in between customers.

She just smiled back at me, sort of serenely, and shook her head. With her left hand she stirred the cep mushrooms in a pan, tossing their smooth brown caps around in the oil, as she stirred the beetroot soup with her right. She would stuff the dumplings with the mushrooms later. Meanwhile, Michal was stuffing cabbage leaves with dried ceps and deftly serving customers in between. 'God is Born' seemed to be playing on a loop behind me and

I realised that we had all managed to bring a little bit of Poland with us. Right here to South Belfast. Mrs Domanska and all the other customers of Michal's shop found a little bit of the 'old country' right here, every day. The food, the language, the customs, the banter – they were all here. Michal had gifted us with a little piece of home that made us all miss Poland that little bit less.

I threw down my drying cloth and ran upstairs to see if Dziadek was awake. I didn't want him to miss out on this atmosphere. I called out for Toni to help me, even though he was still limping quite badly.

'Dziadek, are you asleep?' I asked, stepping into the room.

And just like every other day over the past month it was like he was sitting waiting for me.

'How many days, Magda?' he asked.

'I don't know – I've forgotten, Dziadek,' I lied. 'Why don't you come down to the shop and ask Mama?'

His eyes were the bluest I'd ever seen them.

'Don't be stupid, Magda. Dziadek can't make it all the way downstairs,' said Toni, hobbling in after me.

'Yes, I think I can,' Dziadek answered, his eyes widening. 'I think I can.'

It must have taken at least half an hour to get him

down two flights of stairs. There wasn't much room for Toni's bulk, with Dziadek and me squeezed at his side. A few times I thought Dziadek was going to tumble but he kept talking about the New Year and how things would be different and that seemed to spur him on.

Toni shouted ahead for someone to get a chair ready and when we nearly collapsed into the sweet-smelling shop, Colin pushed one towards Dziadek. He buckled and fell back onto it and looked all around him. He caught Mama's bewildered eyes over in the corner and smiled.

'Chopping more beetroots, Katarina?' he asked.

'Yes, Papa,' she answered, coming towards him and kneeling down. 'It's so good to see you downstairs in the middle of all this!' She swept her arms around the shop which was buzzing and smelling of Christmas. 'Thank you, children, for bringing him down.'

Mama looked up at Toni and me, her eyes glazed with tears.

'How on earth did you manage to get him out of his room?' she asked, almost laughing.

'Sometimes, a person can do things that seem impossible,' Dziadek answered.

He looked around him, at Colin who had come back in, at the customers chattering away to Michal, at the window decorated with tinsel and holly. Outside, passers-by were scurrying along, probably last-minute shopping like their lives depended upon it.

Then, staring into the corner where Mama had been working, Dziadek's eyes seemed to squint into something more serious.

'Roots are important, my daughter,' he said to Mama, looking again at the chopped beetroots. 'Especially at Christmas,' he nodded. 'And always.'

I felt him squeezing my hand and right then and there I was so proud of this old man. And my eyes were glazed now too – with onions and tears.

Apart from Toni's unusual quietness, it may just have been our best ever Christmas in Belfast. Dziadek didn't make it out to church, but he did join us for Christmas dinner and ate more heartily than I'd seen in a long time. Michal and his wife joined us too and somehow the size of our little kitchen didn't matter for once. We still had carp, but only as a starter this time. Instead Mama roasted a turkey for main course, deciding that it was a good thing to blend old and new traditions. The turkey looked as good as the ones in the TV ads – and tasted even better. And *of course* there were potatoes: golden, roast potatoes *and* the mashed variety. Toni had bought crackers for us all to pull: another new 'thing' for us at Christmas. The daft jokes inside even made my brother smirk once or twice, but it was obvious that there was still something bothering him. Only the sight of Modesta arriving at our door in the evening really lifted his spirits. She was really shy at first with Mama and Tata but, as they chatted away to her in Polish, she started to look more at ease.

Mama had decorated the tiny mantelpiece with holly and ivy entwined with red and white Christmas lights and, as the dusk deepened and the lights glowed, I felt as warm inside as I'd ever felt in my new country. Tata poured some fruit *kompot* into glasses and I watched as my family sat back, chatted and relaxed while the fire hissed and muttered in the hearth. The day had been a blend of cultures and I reckoned that's what I was now – a blend. And it really wasn't such a bad thing. And just to make everything almost perfect, it started to snow over the Belfast hills in the distance, soft swirls spooling down outside our window, making me both homesick and *at* home. Looking out over the redbrick houses and deserted streets, I found myself thinking of Colin and what kind of Christmas he was having. He'd been so pleased when Michal had given him his wages the day before. I just hoped that his family were trying as hard as mine to make Christmas special. I didn't dare think about what kind of Christmas Sophie was having. I had a feeling that she was going to bring something new to the mix in the New Year – and I dreaded what that *something* might be. So I put her out of my mind and savoured what was right here in front of me: family, friends and home. And what was that Dziadek had said about roots? I lifted my own glass of *kompot* and remembered Babcia and all the other family members we had left behind. And I decided that next year – next year I would be called Magda, at home *and* at school.

Chapter seventeen

On the first day of the New Year I woke up to a bitingly cold Belfast, mired in freezing fog. Our flat wasn't really equipped for below-zero temperatures so I made up a tray of porridge and hot tea for Dziadek and carried it quickly upstairs, hoping he'd kept his electric blanket on. But, instead of sitting up and waiting for me like he had been doing for weeks now, he was asleep. I knew as soon as I set foot through the door that something had shifted. Dziadek's breathing was coming out in slow rattles and his chest seemed to take an age to rise and fall.

'*Mama! Tata!*' I shouted, setting the tray aside and rushing over to him.

His face was as grey as the Belfast sky. I screamed

again for someone to come and by the time all four of us were in the room his eyes had opened wide again and he looked like he was smiling at some invisible thing at the end of his bed.

'What's wrong with him, Mama?'

Instead of answering me she walked softly towards him, taking his withery hand in hers.

'Is it time, Papa?' she asked him.

'Time for what?' I asked. What the heck was she talking about?

'Say goodbye to your grandfather, Toni and Magda,' she said as if she hadn't even heard me.

'Why? Where is he going?' I squealed.

I searched Tata's face for some clue. He just stood behind Mama, rubbing her arm and nodding his head.

'Dziadek! Dziadek!' I kept crying, but my voice sounded like I was underwater. My parents looked as if everything was normal. Even Toni seemed calm, bending down and kissing Dziadek's forehead.

Tata walked to the other side of the bed now and took Dziadek's other hand, covering it with both of his. Despite the icy temperature in the room they all just seemed so *composed*! Why was no-one phoning an ambulance? Why were they just letting him *go*? But even before I got these questions out, Dziadek took one last deep breath and then just froze.

And was gone.

For I don't know how many minutes it felt like we were all in a bubble. My voice wouldn't work, my hands wouldn't move. I wanted to reach out and touch him, but I didn't want to feel death. Maybe if I closed my eyes, this would all go away? Dziadek would open his eyes again and smile.

All of a sudden, I felt like my heart was taking up too much space in my body, as if my lungs and limbs and brain couldn't function because they were being squeezed so hard. I could hear someone howling like a wounded animal, but it was me that Mama was shushing, comforting. I had never seen anyone die – until now. Thirteen years of friendship had just evaporated with a last breath.

Later Mama told me how she tried to peel me off Dziadek, but Tata had told her to let me hold on for as long as I wanted to. I knew it was because he had known that soon his father-in-law would be ash-skinned and blue-lipped and he would no longer be my granddad. So I clung on to his body, still warm, until the ambulance arrived and took him away, no blue lights flashing, just driving carefully through South Belfast streets. And I realised I would never, ever hear his voice again. There would be no more words for me to listen to on the rare days we went outside. Words that used to surface, glass-bright, with wisdom and something more. Understanding.

On the third day after his death, we carried Dziadek out of the flat in a rich, mahogany coffin; a coffin 'fit for a prince', Mama said. Every Polish person we knew walked silently behind us as we weaved in and out through the streets to St Patrick's Parish Church. As was the custom, only the men carried the coffin, but as we drew nearer to the church I begged Tata to let me help carry it. Tata nodded and I took my place in front of him. I was too short, though, for the coffin to rest on my shoulder so I raised a hand to hold its edge and put the other flat against the base. It was as if I could feel my beloved Dziadek inside.

The ground was covered in frost but I felt as sure-footed as if I was walking on dry concrete. Then, as we moved into the church, I nearly fell over with embarrassment when I saw the Guard of Honour from Belview College: Ann, Emma, Mia, Chloe, Melissa – I counted them off in shock as I passed them. No Sophie though. Then in the sombre darkness inside I noticed Colin sitting alone in the back row, looking up sadly from his pew. I was kind of glad he was there. I hadn't seen him since Christmas Eve. Michal must have told him about Dziadek.

The priest muttered prayers and blessings and spoke of Dziadek's life in Masuria, but at least half of it passed me by. The sweet, smoky smell of incense was starting to make me feel nauseous. Mama had to tap me more than once to stand up and sit down at the right intervals. She had been so *together* through all this – I just couldn't understand it. At least Tata and Toni had shed some tears. Mama shook hands with people as she left the church as if it was a day of no real significance, as if our family hadn't just lost a limb. I couldn't help it, but I could feel myself growing angry with her as she smiled at one sympathiser or another. Nicola – Sophie's mum – stepped up to Mama and offered her condolences, then took both of my hands in hers for a moment. I noticed Modesta's arm linked with Toni's as we followed them to the funeral car.

On the journey to the crematorium I felt like I was holding my breath. I was terrified that if I spoke I would say things that I might regret. I wanted to throw words like knives. I wanted to ask why we hadn't called an ambulance sooner that morning, or how Mama seemed to know it was going to happen, or why she was so bloody *calm!* I wanted her to bark out sobs and flail her arms about in grief, instead of sitting there, her head held high, watching Belfast streets pass us by. Tata held her hand and Toni wept quietly, blowing his nose every few minutes in embarrassment. Why were we all so *accepting* of this?

Dziadek's favourite Polish hymn played in the crematorium and the priest spoke again about him. He seemed a bit less formal now. He spoke of Dziadek returning to his beloved wife and 'everlasting life'. The room smelt polished and woody and sort of cosy compared to the church. There were snowdrops beside the coffin – *the first sign of new life*, Dziadek used to say. I nearly choked on the irony. I tried to remember their botanical name. He had told me that it was a Greek word and that it meant milk and flower, but it wouldn't come back to me. I felt like kicking the floor in frustration.

The curtain opened and the coffin slid through as another of Dziadek's favourites played – 'Nearer My God to Thee' (back in Masuria we used to sing it in Polish) – and he was gone. We sat in stiff silence as he literally just slipped away from us. Michal and his family, Modesta and a few others sat in rows behind us, their bodies taut with respect and grief. I couldn't stand it any more. I ran outside into the biting cold where I sank against a wall, my whole body shaking as if it was going to explode. By the time Mama came out to me I was like a ragged bundle, all elbows and bent back, sobbing like a new-born.

'Magda, it's OK, my love,' she hushed. 'Dziadek is happy – he's going home.'

'*I don't know if I believe in all that crap!*' I screamed. '*How do we know there is a home up there?*' I pointed heavenward. '*How do we know he's going anywhere?*'

'Because we're taking him *home*, Magda. *Home* to Poland.'

'What?'

'We're going to scatter his ashes in the lake where he grew up. Where Babcia's ashes are too.' Mama looked up skywards now too. 'I don't know if there is truly an afterlife either, Magda. I hope there is. But for now, we must believe in our *former* life, and that is Masuria. And that is where your granddad wanted to go. We leave tomorrow, my love, and the whole family will be there to greet us. We will have another small ceremony with them and then together, we will *all* say goodbye.'

I folded myself into her, my shrill crying subsiding into softer sobs. I thought my heart was literally cracking in two.

Chapter eighteen

At Heathrow we changed over to Aeroflot to fly to Kaliningrad in Russia. As the plane spun deep into the night, for the first time since Dziadek's death I fell sound asleep. My dreams were a mash-up of snowdrops and beetroots and Dziadek's map of Poland. I jolted and fell with the dips of the jet, waking finally with my eyes wide and a blanket over my knees.

'We're nearly there, my love,' Mama said. She had sat beside me throughout the flight and Toni and Tata had sat in front. 'What do you remember? About Poland?'

'Most of it,' I shrugged. 'But maybe not all the words. What if there are things I can't say, Mama?'

'Your family will always understand you, Magda,' she said, ruffling my hair like she used to do when I was a child. 'Language does not always have to be *spoken*.'

I wasn't entirely sure what she meant but some of my nerves started to abate as the plane began to slowly descend. Dziadek's ashes were in a zipped bag in the overhead compartment and I was a bit panicky about them falling out and blowing all over the plane on landing.

Kaliningrad Airport was bathed in a weird winter light as we blearily stepped outside into a Minus 5 temperature. A taxi-bus pulled alongside the pavement by Arrivals and we jumped in out of the cold, Mama carrying the bag with the ashes carefully.

I screwed my eyes into a squint in the early morning light, driving along what was a wedge-shaped piece of land between Poland and Lithuania. It was the same place we had flown out from, nearly five years ago when we had emigrated. Tata always said Kaliningrad didn't know what it was, Russian or Polish. Some of its people might even have seen themselves as German. I remembered thinking that it sounded as mixed up as good old Northern Ireland.

When we reached Gizycko, Uncle Pawel, Mama's brother, was standing with his arms held wide like he was ready to catch something falling from the sky. Mama fell into them and for the first time since Dziadek's death she cried and cried. Other brothers and sisters moved in and joined in the embrace and I was looking at my mum in a different way. I could see her now as the 'baby' of the family, being comforted and consoled by her elders. Maybe she had saved her grief for this moment? I suppose I had forgotten that our parents are something beyond mothers and fathers. We forget that they are little sisters and beloved daughters. Tata, Toni and I stood back and let her mourn with her family for as long as she needed to.

Inside Uncle Pawel's house there was barely room to move. Aunts, uncles, cousins, neighbours that I hadn't seen in so long, all gathered together to remember Dziadek. And for a moment I felt guilty that I had hoarded my grief all to myself. All of these people would miss him – *had* been missing him – as much as I would.

Aunt Weronika called us to the table and then Pawel cleared his throat, ready to say a few words about his father. The *stypa* – the wake – was important to the family, a chance to remember Dziadek as a group and to celebrate his life. No food would be eaten until Uncle Pawel had traced his father's life in words and commemorated him.

There was standing room only as my extended family hovered in the kitchen, the hallway and even the front room that looked out over the lake.

Pawel and Weronika lived a little bit up from the port, on a hill of red-roofed houses with buttermilk-coloured walls, but almost everywhere you looked in Gizycko you could see water or trees. My granddad had missed this place so much and I realised I had too. Uncle Pawel had started saying a decade of the Rosary and I fumbled in my pocket for my beads, sweating a little at the thought that I could barely remember how to say it in Polish. My curious-eyed cousins all muttered away in unison, glancing at me from time to time when I forgot the words. Dziadek had told me more than once not to spit on my roots, but that was complicated when you were trying to be Maggie, flying under the radar in Belview College and trying your damndest not to get a word wrong in English. Remembering the rosary in Polish had just *not* been a priority! Dominika, the cousin closest in age to me, smiled over at me with something like understanding.

After we all said *Amen*, Weronika pointed to the plates and told us to help ourselves. We circled round the table, lifting potato and ham *perogie*, grilled *kielbasa* (sausages), boiled cauliflower with broad beans and a dozen other Polish specialities.

At least the food wasn't lost to me, as Mama cooked most of this at home. But as the family chatted and bantered, I knew I could no longer fit in completely. At least a quarter of what they were saying went over my head and I just wanted to escape. Everyone was as welcoming and as lovely as I expected, but I was back to feeling like a blend that was neither one thing nor the other.

Toni found me outside about half an hour later. I was hunched down on the ground in front of my uncle's bungalow, watching people idle along the promenade below. The lake, which had been frozen the week before, was bordered by forests of pine trees and the air felt as fresh as I remembered it. A single sail creaked on the wind. No anti-Polish graffiti on walls or hooded youths throwing stones. Why the heck did we ever leave?

'Cousin Oskar was saying that over a million workers earn less than the minimum wage in Poland,' Toni said, as if reading my mind and answering my question as he slid down beside me.

'Yeah, but at least you get to be *somebody* here. Tata would still be a teacher and not a gardener!'

'There's nothing wrong with being a gardener, Magda. Tata loves his job, can't you see that? He loves being outdoors, not inside a classroom with squabbling teenagers.'

'He didn't go to university to become a *gardener*!' I spat out. 'He's better than that!'

'Who do you think you are, Magda?' Toni turned on me angrily. 'You have turned into such a little snob since we moved to Belfast! Why can't you look beyond yourself and think about other people for a change!'

'What do you mean?'

'I mean it's all about *poor* Magda, having to put up with a disappointment of a brother and a father who get their hands dirty at work,' he said, getting up and moving away from me. 'You never think of anything else but *your* problems!' His face was fury red as he spat these words at me.

I couldn't remember a time ever before when Toni had been this angry at me. Usually *I* was the one doing the shouting.

'We've *all* had to make adjustments to our lives since living in Ireland – not just you,' he went on, raking his fingers through his hair. 'But you mope around like the world owes you a favour, playing the victim all the time. Maybe if you smiled once or twice people might actually like you!'

Now *that* was below the belt! I felt my stomach lurch as my big brother raged at me as if he hated me. There was something in his eyes that I'd never seen before – contempt. It scared the living daylights out of me.

'Toni, I … I'm sorry. I–I didn't know you felt like this,' I stammered, getting up and walking towards him.

'Of course you didn't,' he said, more softly now. 'Because you've been so caught up in how the move to Ireland was difficult for *you*. It was difficult for all of us, Magda, but wake up and smell the coffee – or whatever it is they say in Belfast – because we *had* to move away from Poland. Tata had lost his job, Magda. And he nearly lost himself too. We kept that from you.'

He came over to me now and hugged me.

'What … what do you mean?' I asked.

'There were redundancies in the school. So many children were leaving to emigrate with their families and they just had too many staff. And there weren't any more jobs to be found.' He pulled me close to him. 'I'm sure you know what Tata is like when he's not busy, Magda. He was falling into a kind of depression.'

'I … I didn't realise,' I hiccupped, crying into his warm, thick jumper now. 'I didn't know.'

'There are a lot of things you don't know, Magda,' he said, peering down at me. 'You don't know how Mama will suffer now without her father. You don't know how upset Tata is that he embarrasses you in school. And you don't know that I see the way you look at me, like I'm a moron.' He let go of me and

181

walked away, shoving his hands in his pockets. 'But at least you got *that* one right, because I am!'

'Toni, don't say that!' I begged him, running after him and trying to turn him round. 'You're my big brother and I love you and admire you.'

'Well, you won't admire me when you hear what I've done. What Sophie's done. Let's put it this way, when I get back to Belfast, I won't have a job. I won't be in Belview College to embarrass you any more.'

'What the ...? What are you talking about?'

'The day I went to Sophie's house? Her dad wasn't there. Her mum wasn't there. Just Sophie – in her bedroom.'

I knew I was going to heave right there and then. The story that I'd been dreading was about to come out.

Aunt Weronika's smoked herring came up my throat and spewed out all over her front yard.

Toni waited until evening when we were back in the Hotel Europa to tell me the whole story. Mama was exhausted from the emotion of the day and had gone to her room with Tata. Toni and I hugged mugs of tea in the cream-walled lobby. There was no-one behind Recepcia and, with the shiny floor tiles and only Toni and I around, our voices seemed to echo and bounce off the walls.

'What the heck were you thinking?' I asked him.

'I wasn't thinking. I just … I don't know, I thought I was there to pick up tiles. Sophie answered the door and said that her dad wasn't home and that the tiles were upstairs. I know how bloody stupid it sounds, but I just didn't realise what was happening.'

'But I *warned* you about Sophie,' I said, spilling hot tea on the tips of my fingers. 'I told you to be careful with her!'

'I had no idea what she was going to turn into!' He put his mug down and paced about the empty lobby. 'I went upstairs to collect a box of tiles and she pointed to a door and said they were in that room. When I walked in all I could see was a bed with the covers turned down.'

'Shit, Toni! I don't think I even want to hear this,' I said, putting the mug down and burying my head in my hands.

'I asked her where her dad was. She just said he'd gone out. So I asked her where her mum was and she started raving and shouting about Charlie someone. Then she started sobbing and I sat down beside her on the edge of the bed and put my arm around her. I know – I know! If I could turn the clock back …'

He slid to the floor and sobbed into his hands. I was thanking my lucky stars that there were no other guests around.

Even though I could barely catch a breath, I asked him as calmly as I could about what happened next.

'She pulled me closer to her and the next thing I knew she was kissing me. I pulled back but she grabbed me again and pulled me on top of her.'

'Toni, you're a *big* lad, how could you let Sophie pull you down?'

'She's a girl, Magda – I didn't want to be rough with her and push her off!' he cried, crossing his arms on his knees like he used to do when he was a little boy.

'Then what?' I asked, my voice barely a whisper. I walked to the window and could just about see the hills on the far side of the lake. My insides were heaving again.

'Then she took a photograph with her phone,' he answered, and I knew then that we were in real trouble.

My eyes blurred as I tried to focus on the row of pines that staggered on the far slope of the lake. The sun had dipped low now and, through my washed eyes, it looked like the trees were swaying in some sort of weird dance. That's what my relationship with Sophie had been all along: two steps forward and one step back and then she'd whizz me around until I was blinded by her.

'Does she intend to share the photo?' I asked, my voice hollow.

'She already has.'

I threw my arms around him. Toni had been suffering all of this through Christmas and through the funeral and had tried to keep it all in. Not like me – I'd have thrown ten tantrums by now. I had always known my brother was a deep well of kindness, but I never admired him more than at that minute.

'Who?' I stammered. 'Who did she share it with?'

'Someone called Paul?' he said with a question mark. 'For safekeeping, whatever that means.'

Mr Sneer! I remembered him well from that day in Newcastle. But why on earth would she share it with him?

'I still don't get it,' I said, sitting back down on the cold leather sofa. 'She was supposed to be going Christmas shopping that day with her mum.'

'Yeah, she said something about that, but her mum had gone off for the day with Charlie instead.'

'Charlie the gardener?'

Toni shrugged. 'Dunno. Just that Sophie seemed furious about it and she said that her dad had gone nuts about it too.'

'So where was her dad?'

'Apparently he'd gone to find her mum and have it out with her.'

This was all too weird. I knew there were cracks

in that household, but what the heck did Charlie have to do with it all? I remembered the last time I was at their house and Sophie had gone outside and started yelling at Charlie. Which was also weird. What if …?

'I think I need to go to bed now, Magda,' Toni said, pulling himself up. 'I don't know who will have seen the photo by now, but I don't expect to be back in Belview College ever again. Silver linings, eh?' He half-smiled, patting me on the back and walking away.

Poor Toni – trying to make a joke out of the fact that I had never wanted him and Tata at school. What sort of person was I? Was Toni right – was I a bully? I sat there on that faux-leather sofa and listened to the clock tick above the reception desk. No-one had been manning it all evening as far as I could see. The spotlights above my head were starting to make my eyes and head hurt.

What the hell were we going to do? What would Dziadek have said? What advice would he have given? And just as his absence was feeling the strongest I knew strangely that he was here with us. Telling us what to do. It was simple really. *Just tell the truth:* that's what Dziadek would have said.

Chapter nineteen

The next day Aunt Weronika, Uncle Pawel, Dominika and I took a walk down to the Ekomarina at the city dock. The quayside looked really different since I'd last seen it. Lots of new cafés were strung along it now like beads on a necklace. There was a lovely new viewing terrace and a much bigger play area for kids. A handful of yachts bobbed and clinked in the water.

Dominika and I decided to forget that we were teenagers and raced each other to the swings, nearly knocking each other over to get on the Flying Saucer. This big, round basket had always been my favourite, whether lying down or standing up in it.

I hadn't forgotten about last night's conversation

with Toni, but I knew there was nothing we could do about it until we returned to Ireland. So for now I was making the most of my time with my family. It's what Dziadek would have wanted.

'Do you miss being here?' Dominika asked.

'Yes. And no,' I said truthfully. 'Being here makes me realise how Irish I've become. I don't feel that I fit in here completely any more. But then, I feel the opposite way round in Belfast.' I shrugged, letting her push me on the Flying Saucer.

'Is it hard? Fitting in? Speaking another language?'

'Very,' I answered, jumping off now and letting her take her turn on the swing. 'But I think I have probably settled in better than I realised. I miss our house here in Gizycko though, and my friends from school. And family obviously.'

'Do you want to go and see your house? I'm sure we'd be allowed,' she suggested.

I stopped pushing her for a moment and thought about it. Our house was just over a half a mile away in the St Bruno area and we could easily walk to it. Split-level, built in the 1970s, it was the perfect home. We even had a balcony out the back which looked over the lake in the distance and a back yard with a barbeque. We were considered *comfortably* off, not thought of as immigrant trash. Nobody spray-painted our walls or asked if we were *foreign*.

But then again, Tata had become very low here after losing his job, according to Toni. The new start in Belfast had given him a new lease of life. And it would be hard to find a school as good as Belview College here.

'You know, Dominika,' I said. 'I don't think I do want to see it. That house is part of my past, not my present. I don't think there's any point in torturing myself by looking at something that belongs to another family now.'

My cousin nodded her head, understanding. She was pretty much a taller version of me: same light-brown hair and strong cheekbones, but without the chip on her shoulder. For a split second I nearly thought about changing my mind. I missed the little stream that used to run past our house and down the hill. Toni had taught me how to catch sticklebacks in it – little dark darts quivering out from under the shadows of stones. I remembered putting one in a jam-jar filled with water from the stream – and the next morning it was white and shiny and dead. I must have been about six at the time, a young age to learn that life could be crap sometimes.

'What about seeing old friends then?' Dominika asked, pushing her ponytail into her bobble hat.

'Yes, maybe. Let's just enjoy this for now,' I said,

glancing around at people ambling along the quayside, wrapped up in heavy coats against the winter sun. Tilting my head to the sky, feeling the beaded mist of spray from the water skiers coming close to the edge of the lake, I decided this was enough for now.

Dominika and I huddled along together towards the jetty, looking out across the swelling water below where we had scattered Dziadek's ashes. I could almost feel the lake breathing on me in the light wind and I closed my eyes and felt my granddad near me. Dominika linked my arm and we both just stood there for ages: watching, listening. Bold, beady-eyed gulls hovered above us, obviously looking for crumbs to peck on.

'Come on, let's walk again,' she said eventually. 'I've lost all feeling in my fingers and toes!'

'I know!' I said. 'Let's go to our old primary school.'

'Yeah, why not?' she laughed. 'You know how I was a year above you? Well, I was always under strict instructions from Mama and Tata to keep an eye out for you,' she said, rolling her eyes. 'As if you needed *anyone* keeping an eye on you!'

'Really? I didn't know that,' I said, giggling. 'I always thought you were just spying on me so you could tell Uncle Pawel and Aunt Weronika about what I was doing wrong. You know, you were a bit *stern*, Dominika.' I pulled off her bobble hat and ran away with it, laughing my head off. 'I always thought you needed to lighten up!' I called back.

She chased after me. 'Is this light enough?' she shouted, wrenching the hat off me and knocking me to the grassy verge, ticking me like I was a toddler.

Yesterday the grass blades had been standing like white spears, but they were starting to let go of the frost now. I laughed until my face must have been the colour of a beetroot. Nobody played like this at Belview College. Nobody.

'Mind you, you're the one who seems stern these days,' Dominika said, helping me up. 'I know you're grieving – we all are – but you seem … different.'

I nodded my head, knowing exactly what she meant. Belfast had hardened me and not necessarily in a good way.

As we arrived at the gates of Szkola Podstawowa, I saw the fat, white-washed building from my childhood. There was a snake chalked out in the playground, just visible beneath the thin frost, and the sycamore tree that used to drop its 'helicopters' in the autumn. The gate creaked open and we went towards the cloakrooms where pipes used to creak all winter and probably still did.

'Do you remember Miss Dabrowska?' Dominika

asked. 'She used to have a globe at the front of her classroom that she was always spinning.'

I did remember. I remembered her painted nails pointing to countries like France and Germany – and Ireland. I remembered thinking how small Ireland looked as I sat cross-legged on carpet tiles.

'She was the nicest teacher,' Dominika was saying as we walked round the back of the building, glancing in through windows.

But I had sort of stopped listening, because I was right back there in my first classroom, other children flapping around me with crusty noses and an alphabet on the board that made no sense. The teacher reading nursery rhymes that actually frightened me and the carpet tiles scratching my legs.

'Magda? Anybody in there?' Dominika knocked at my head.

'It just seems so long ago,' I whispered. 'Dziadek or Babcia used to pick us from school – remember? They'd have to go backwards and forwards to collect us all at different times.'

There were six of us in that school at the same time, all cousins. Our granddad and grandma were our main carers during the day while our parents worked. Mama had worked part-time in a bakery in Grunwaldzki Square but, out of all our aunts and uncles, she was the one who spent the most time with our grandparents. She cleaned for them and cooked for them quite often too. In fact, she was probably around enough to pick me up from school but somehow Dziadek always claimed that role.

'So what is it, then? What's making you so ... anxious?' Dominika asked as we walked back to her house through streets lined with apartment blocks.

Every balcony was bedecked with winter flowers in window boxes. Some blocks were shabbier than others, but even those had an old-world charm about them with their peeling cream paint and terracotta roof tiles.

'Come on, I'm your big cousin,' she said, taking my hand. 'Spill.'

So I told her everything, and at times it was hard to find the words in Polish to describe my relationship with Sophie. I told her all about the stone-throwing, school, our tatty flat, *everything*. We were almost back at Uncle Pawel's by the time I had finished.

'So what are you going to do?' she asked.

'Go back – take the rough with the smooth. Pray that Toni keeps his job. To make the most of it, I suppose.'

'You know that Gizycko will *always* be your second home, Magda. We're all here for you. But you're right. Belfast is where you need the make the best of things. And it doesn't sound *all* bad – Michal's shop, the Mourne Mountains, your school – even that Colin guy.'

She put her arm round me and told me about the opportunities I would have in Ireland that I might not have in Poland.

'But Poland's always waiting for you. If you need to come back.'

She was right. I had two worlds to choose from. Part of me just wished for one plain life, with no choices in it. Like a lake stretching out as far as you could see, just water for mile after mile. But that wasn't my reality. My reality was Radlan Street and Dominika had helped me to see that. Our breath fogged on the air now as the temperatures started to drop again, but *something* had warmed up inside me. And I knew I was ready to go home.

Chapter twenty

The slice and whip of the wind was shredding the skin off Belfast Lough. Mama, Tata, Toni and I were standing at the water's edge in the Titanic Quarter, feeling the salt spray mists against our faces. Mama hadn't told us until today that she had kept some of Dziadek's ashes back. She wanted to scatter some here in Belfast, so that any time she looked out to the lough she could feel close to him.

'You know, he never even got to visit this,' Mama said, pointing at the *Titanic* Museum as we walked towards it.

'You know Dziadek,' I laughed. 'He only liked museums that were *free*.'

And the *Titanic* Museum certainly wasn't free. As

one of the top visitor attractions in Ireland, I supposed it had the right to charge the amount that it did but, for a family of five, it had always been too expensive for us. Now that we were a family of *four*, Tata decided it was time that we went inside.

'Papa would have enjoyed it, you know,' he said as we walked through the glass-fronted entrance. 'He was interested in maritime history. And there's no bigger maritime story than the *Titanic*.'

My granddad had loved stories, but he hadn't really embraced Ireland's stories, and I was coming to realise that they were as rich and fascinating as our native folklore from Poland. Walking through the galleries learning about the *Titanic*'s construction and launch – and then her tragic end – I wished we *had* wheeled Dziadek around all of this. But then, his time had sadly run out. Mine hadn't. And I was determined to find out more about life in this corner of the world.

'When are you going back to school?' Toni asked me as we stared at the 'grave' of the *Titanic* under the glass floor. A camera panned over her watery grave beneath our feet.

'Monday. Mama said that would be time enough,' I explained.

'I think I'll go and see Mrs Walsh tomorrow,' he said, sliding his hands into his pockets with a sigh.

'She's bound to know about the photo and I need to put things right.'

'Well, she hasn't been in touch with us, except to pass on her condolences, so maybe she doesn't know anything?'

'Doesn't matter, Magda. I need to tell her. And I need to tell Tata.'

I nodded my head, understanding his need to come clean. It was a surreal conversation to be having, floating above the 'wreck' of the *Titanic*.

'Perhaps Tata should go with you when you speak to her,' I suggested.

'That's what I was hoping for,' Toni nodded. 'And if she sacks me, well, at least I can explain to her that it has nothing to do with my father.'

Looking at Toni now – properly looking – I realised how much weight he had lost in recent weeks. He'd lost that little bit of chubbiness that made him Toni. His cheeks were shallower and his eyes had kind of lost their glint.

'You'll get another job, Toni. I'm sure of it. Especially with you having your own transport.'

'But how will Tata get to work if I have the car? Take the school bus with *you*? That would make you *real* happy,' he scowled.

I felt myself gulping with shame at my attitude towards my family – from now on all that would change. I had made a secret promise to Dziadek that I would be proud of my family and proud of my roots – but at the same time take a chance on the new – embrace my new life too.

Toni dropped us off outside Michal's shop before heading off. He didn't say where he was going, but I had a feeling it was something to do with Modesta. Lurking on the corner of the street was the usual grey hoody.

'Hi, Colin,' I said, walking towards him. 'What's up?'

A shrug. 'Nothin' new. Wanna go for a walk?' He jerked his head in the direction of the main road.

'Yeah, I suppose so. I'll just let Mama and Tata know.'

I told them and Tata said, 'Fine – take care'. I couldn't read Mama's expression.

'How did it go in Poland?' Colin asked a few minutes later, scuffling along beside me.

'Good,' I answered. 'Sad, but good.'

We strolled along the knotted tangle of streets branching off the Donegall Road, flags hanging everywhere. Or *flegs* as they were called round here. They were on every pole and post: red, white and blue fading into green, white and gold, depending on which street we turned into.

'There was someone round your place when you

were away. I was … sort of keepin' an eye out.'

'Who was it?'

Another shrug. 'Some goodlookin' bird. About your age. Think it might have been that friend of yours.'

'Seriously? Bloody hell – she has a nerve!'

'She was inside, talkin' to Michal,' Colin went on, ignoring my outburst.

Jesus! Was there no end to her man-baiting? Was she trying to seduce a middle-aged married man now?

'God! I wish she'd leave us alone! I seriously wish I'd never met that girl!'

'I think she was sort of upset,' Colin said, looking at me in confusion. 'Michal was tellin' her you'd all gone away by the time I walked into the shop.'

'Yeah, she'll have been looking for sympathy from Michal about God knows what! Hoping she'd put his arm around her, no doubt!' I spat out.

'Dunno. But she said something about going away. To Thailand.'

'Yeah, that'd be right,' I spluttered. 'Throw a bomb at our family and then clear off after she's caused destruction all around her.'

Colin still looked confused. 'Bomb? Why would she be carryin' a bomb?'

'No, I don't mean *literally*. Never mind. I'll find

out all about what she's been up to on Monday,' I said, my stomach sinking again. 'If not sooner.'

'Wanna chip?' Colin asked, changing the subject. 'My treat?'

'Sure. Why not?'

I knew that Colin had been working round the clock at Michal's place but I still didn't know how he got away with staying off school. I *did* know that he didn't want me to keep asking.

'I've stopped the fegs,' he said proudly, handing over change to the man in the chippy van. Fags, he meant.

'Brilliant!' I said, thinking how much healthier he looked. He had lost the gaunt look too, and his green eyes had a brightness about them now. We tucked into the warm, salty chips which I was really beginning to get a taste for.

'Thought maybe you mightn't have come back,' Colin said between mouthfuls, looking down at the ground.

'Well, we did. We're here in Belfast and we're here to stay.' Looking up at the Belfast mountains in the distance, I figured there were worse places to live.

'There won't be any more graffiti though. Or stones,' Colin said under his breath.

'How come?'

The usual shrug. 'I told someone about it. And they told someone else. And they said it's not gonna happen any more.'

What the heck? My blood felt like it had run cold.

'Do you *know* people, Colin?' I asked, not quite sure I wanted to hear the answer. 'Like, know a certain *sort* of people?'

'No. But my brother does. I don't normally have anythin' to do with him. But I wanted you to come back. So I asked him to sort it.' He was looking me in the eye now which was a pretty rare thing for Colin.

I wasn't sure whether to be terrified about this revelation or touched.

'I'm gonna keep workin' at Michal's,' he went on, as if he hadn't just declared his connections with the *underworld*. 'He says he's gonna take me on properly when I'm finished school. Then I'm gonna move out. Away from my brother. Away from my da.'

He turned away from me now, obviously having had enough eye contact for the day.

Crikey – people had mixed-up lives in this city! Sophie in her Chester Road mansion, pretending her life was perfect, and Colin with a family he wanted to be rid of. But then again, imperfect families lived everywhere – not just in Belfast.

Colin seemed like he was only warming up as he

started to tell me more and more about his family. He hadn't seen his mum in three years and had no idea where she was, but he was glad she was gone.

'Why?' I asked.

'Because wherever she is, she's safe. From Da,' he said, swiping the last of his chips through the blob of tomato ketchup. 'I hope she's livin' by the sea somewhere, or tucked away in the mountains. Happy. I'm gonna find her when I'm older. And then we'll both be happy.'

He nodded his head before binning his rubbish, pleased with his plan by the look of him.

'And you're gonna be happy too, Magda. I know it,' he said, smiling.

'You reckon?' I asked, smiling back.

'I reckon,' he said, looking at me again like he was studying a specimen in a jar. A nice specimen.

Chapter twenty-one

Mrs Walsh hadn't been available for Toni to speak to, so when I arrived into school on Monday I hadn't a clue what my family and I were going to face. The first thing that I *did* face was the return of Miss Kennedy: The Wicked Witch.

'Welcome back, Magda,' she said to me. 'I'm only just back a few days myself so we'll get used to things together.'

Was Miss Kennedy actually being nice? She was walking along the corridor with me like we were besties.

'Has … has Mr Mawhinney gone then?' I dared to ask.

'No, Mrs Walsh has kept him on. But he's being

allocated to a different form class now. I'm afraid you're stuck with me.' And she actually *smiled*! 'Could you come and see me in my room for a few minutes at lunchtime?'

'Erm, yes, Miss,' I answered, dreading being alone with the Wicked Witch.

'Now, I just need to pop to the staffroom and then I'll be up to take registration,' she said over her shoulder to me, moving briskly along the corridor.

'Hi, Maggie,' said Anna, coming towards me as Miss Kennedy walked away. I saw she had *two* schoolbags slung over her shoulders. She was always afraid she'd forget something, so she literally packed every single book every single day.

'You're back,' she added, stating the very obvious. 'Sorry about your granddad.'

'Thanks, Anna,' I said, genuinely touched. 'And thanks for being in the Guard of Honour at the funeral. Oh, and it's Magda now, by the way.'

'*Okaaay*,' she said, unsure of this change. She blew at her thick fringe and asked if she could walk me to my form room.

'It was weird being without you in Science. I was a bit like Billy-no-mates,' she said, muttering under her fringe.

Jesus! Anna had found a sense of humour since I'd been away!

'And with Sophie gone too, of course,' she added.

'Gone?' I stopped in my tracks outside G18. 'Gone where?'

'Gone to Thailand. Didn't you know?'

'For a holiday?' I asked, afraid to hear the answer.

'Not for a holiday, Maggie,' she said, her fringe shaking. 'She's gone for good.'

'*Whaat?*' I'd known it was kind of on the cards, but I never really believed her dad would actually go through with it.

'Yes – her mum and dad had the biggest falling-out ever and he's taken Sophie away from her.'

'Are you sure, Anna?'

'It's true!' Mia Campbell seemed to have appeared out of nowhere, flicking her mane of hair to the side and rolling up her skirt even higher until it barely passed her thighs. 'My mum knows all about it because she knows the people who own the coffee shop next to Nicola's gallery. Apparently Mr Long said that Nicola was an unfit mother.'

'But that's not true,' I found myself saying, pushing the door into G18 open and going in.

'Not according to Ben Long,' said Mia, as she and Anna followed me to my desk.

I threw my bag down on my chair.

Mia slipped herself onto the corner of my desk – a place where she had *never* sat before. Another flick of the shiny hair and she prepared herself to spill some more.

'Nicola had been having an affair with the gardener!' she crowed with a grin, enjoying spreading the gossip. 'Imagine – the bloody gardener! And she hadn't been keeping an eye on Sophie's progress at school. It's true – Mum's friend heard it all through the gallery wall. Ben was shouting like a madman and said he was taking Sophie to live in Thailand. Nicola was *screaming* at him!'

I wondered for a minute if this was some sort of Mia wind-up. 'Poor Nicola,' I said, almost under my breath. 'What a horrible thing to do to her – to take her daughter away.'

'Well, she should have thought of that before acting like a hussy,' Chloe joined in. 'Anyway, Sophie thought she was better than the rest of us. We're well rid of her.'

'I thought you were her friends,' I said, looking at the pair of them with their bunched-up skirts and thick-pencilled eyebrows. 'How can you be so mean?'

'*Mean?*' screeched Mia. 'You weren't exactly her best mate – always falling out with her and stuff!'

'There was something about her I didn't trust,' I muttered. 'But we can't bitch about her now, because she's gone – she's not here to defend herself.'

The two of them rolled their eyes in unison and abandoned me, obviously realising I wasn't going to add fuel to their fire of gossip.

Miss Kennedy came in and called the roll, read out notices and said the morning prayer. And then she started talking to us – not *at* us – but to us.

'I know I've been back a few days, ladies, but I haven't felt like I could really explain my absence until now.'

She coughed, actually seemed unsure of herself. She was still pencil-slim but her edges seemed to have softened a little.

'I took time off to be with my father,' she said. 'He … he was dying. And I felt that the least he deserved was that I be with him until he passed.'

She dropped her head and I thought she was going to cry. She didn't much look like a wicked witch right then.

'I had the privilege of spending every day with him for the past few months, revisiting the past … recalling memories,' she said, raising her head and staring out through the window as if she could see him out there. 'And I can't tell you how important that was, girls. To really *be with* a family member that you love in their last part of the journey of life.'

She turned back to us now, her eyes glazed.

'Treasure it, girls. Treasure your families – because they won't be with you forever.'

And she glanced at me with some sort of knowing. And I knew that I had been lucky to be with Dziadek until the end. And I knew that I was lucky every single day with the family that I had, both here and in Poland. Luckier than Colin, luckier than Sophie, and luckier than so many other people.

'Thanks for calling in, Magda. Take a seat.'

Miss Kennedy pointed to a chair beside her desk. She finished shuffling some papers then turned to me. Her mid-brown hair was shorter than it used to be, more of a bob-length now. Neat and serious.

'I just wanted to say that I'm here for you – if you need me. Mrs Walsh has made me aware of how close you were to your grandfather, and about your trip back to Poland to bring him home. It can't be easy for you, coming back to school with all that pain tucked away.'

She spoke as if she really understood, as if she really knew me.

'I haven't been as supportive of you girls as I should have been,' she went on, taking her glasses off now. 'And I haven't been as supportive of *you*, Magda, as I should have. Moving here from a different country, having to adapt – I should have been more appreciative of how that must have been for you.'

'It's – it's OK. Honestly,' I said, feeling embarrassed by all this *niceness*, pushing a strand of hair behind my ear like I always did when I was uncomfortable.

'It's not OK,' she insisted, waving her glasses around. 'My father made me see that. I had become too concerned with paperwork and forgot about *pupil*work.' She smiled, liking her own wordplay. 'But that's all going to change.' She brushed something invisible off her skirt and looked like she meant business. 'And I want to start with *listening*. I want to know what's troubling you, Magda.'

'Troubling me? N-nothing,' I said. 'Apart from missing my granddad.'

'I know that, but, there's something else as well, isn't there?'

She looked right into my eyes like she knew. Knew everything.

I could feel my heart start to palpitate at the thought of telling her about my whole friendship journey with Sophie, about my suspicions, about Toni. About everything.

Her green eyes were still focused on me, so I took the deepest of breaths and told her the whole sorry lot of it. Right from the beginning.

Chapter twenty-two

Mrs Walsh's office felt crammed. Me, Toni and Tata sat in front of her, and Miss Kennedy at the side. Nicola Long was at the other side. Toni had gone through the whole story, with Mrs Walsh interrupting every now and again to get her facts right. She wrote *everything* down. She asked Mrs Long to verify if Sophie was in the house on the day of the 'occurrence'.

'Yes,' she said, smudging tears away from underneath her eyeliner. 'I was in Bangor. With Charlie,' she said, rolling her eyes. 'I was supposed to go shopping with Sophie and I let her down. She was so cross with me that she told her daddy all kinds of spiteful things.' Her had voice started to crack.

I could feel Toni shift beside me, could sense his discomfort. Tata's jaw was slack with incomprehension.

'Charlie was – is – my friend. Nothing more, nothing less. But I shouldn't have let Sophie down that day. It was the promise of an original Bevan Gallagher painting that lured me to Bangor with Charlie – nothing else.'

'Mrs Long, you don't have to tell us any of this. We're just interested in the facts behind the alleged photograph,' Mrs Walsh said sympathetically.

It was an 'alleged' photograph because, amazingly, no-one had seen it. Sophie hadn't brought the photo to *anyone's* attention, apparently. Not even Paul, because Nicola had quizzed him about this when the whole matter was reported to her.

'No, I want to explain,' Nicola went on. 'I want to tell you anything that might be relevant to help clear this mess up for Toni. He doesn't deserve this.' She inhaled deeply. 'I'm so sorry, Toni. And Magda. Sorry to your whole family.'

She shook her head and blinked away more tears.

'I knew my daughter could be manipulative – but *this!* This is beyond what I thought she was capable of.'

Her usually neat, shiny bob looked colourless and tired. She had given up on trying to stop her mascara and eyeliner running now, and her pale face was streaked with black.

'We still haven't heard Sophie's account of this, Mrs Long, so we cannot prove that the occurrence didn't take place until we have spoken to her.' Mrs Walsh looked at Nicola and then Toni as she said this, and I knew that she was trying to be as factual as possible about things, but I still wished she could rule Toni out of any wrongdoing right there and then.'As your daughter's principal I have a duty of care to her, Mrs Long, so I must ask you this. Was Sophie taken out of the country without your permission?'

Nicola nodded, her face collapsing into distress. 'When I got back from the gallery last Wednesday, Sophie was gone,' she said, her voice deepening with anger. 'And her passport. Ben had threatened it, but I never thought he would go through with it.'

For the first time in all of this, I felt sorry for Sophie. Had she been a pawn in her parents' ongoing feud? I knew her life wasn't as perfect as it seemed on the surface, but I was only starting to realise how lonely she must have been. Being moved from school to school on her father's whim, shoved on a plane and criss-crossing continents and seas when they had another argument. No wonder she had been so clingy.

Tata had sat silent through all of this, but now the former teacher in him seemed to return. He spoke of Toni's work-ethic and character, and defended him to the hilt while at no time denigrating Sophie. He talked about Sophie's visits to our flat and how lost she always seemed to be. This was news to me. I always thought my family were taken in by her charm.

'She was a classic case of someone wearing their bravado like a shield,' he went on, 'and her ...' He paused.

'Her what, Mr Jankowski?' the principal probed.

'I really don't want to be disrespectful, Mrs Walsh ... Mrs Long,' he said, glancing at Nicola. 'I suppose what I'm trying to say is, that for someone so young, Sophie was quite able to behave in an *amorous* way – almost seductive.'

Bloody hell! I thought. I hadn't even realised he'd noticed.

'Thank you, Mr Jankowski. And thank you to all of you for your accounts of what has been happening,' Mrs Walsh said, peering round the table over her glasses. 'I appreciate Miss Kennedy bringing this whole matter to me in the first place. And I'm sorry for the distress that everyone in this office has been feeling, but you will understand that I still need to speak to Sophie. I fear this is a young woman at risk, and I am genuinely concerned for her welfare.'

My dad and Miss Kennedy nodded. I started to feel a chill, like I needed a warm jumper. I had been so busy hating Sophie at times that I hadn't thought of what *made* her the way she was. I looked up at the wall behind Mrs Walsh and saw one of Sophie's drawings. And then I noticed the replica of Hearst Castle that she had created, on top of a filing cabinet near the window. It was so intricate and detailed. And beautiful. A person who made something like that couldn't be all bad, could they?

'Mr Jankowski, I am so, so sorry about all of this,' Nicola said to Tata as we walked through the school foyer. 'Believe me, I am under no illusions about what Sophie can be capable of.'

She took Tata's hand and shook it and right there and then she looked so pitiful. Not shiny and sleek, but tired and wan.

'But what about you, Mrs Long?' Tata said to her. 'You must be sick with worry. Is there anything we can do?'

Nicola looked almost shy for a moment. 'Would the three of you consider having a coffee with me? I … I just want to talk to someone about all of this. Properly.'

'Of *course* we will, Mrs Long. Magda has been released for the rest of the day and will need a bite to eat anyway. But, please, come back with us to our flat. Nobody makes better coffee than my wife.' He gently touched her shoulder.

'Thank you. And call me Nicola,' she answered, looking at him gratefully. 'I'll be right behind you in the car. I know where Radlan Street is,' she said, glancing at me with half a smile.

'I used to live just three streets away from here,' Nicola said, as she followed Tata and me up the stairs.

Toni had gone for a walk. He said he needed some air.

'A two-up, two-down. Cosy little house it was,' she went on.

I couldn't imagine Nicola in a red-bricked terraced house, but I now knew that not everything was as it seemed with the Longs.

'Do you know?' she said, stepping into our kitchen. 'I was as happy as Larry, swizzing around lamp-posts and playing hopscotch on the streets. Maybe that's where I went wrong with Sophie – not enough outdoorsy getting down and dirty stuff.'

Mama greeted Nicola, sat her down and started to make coffee. Tata had rung ahead and told her we were bringing company home and I could see that she had obviously whizzed the hoover around the place.

'You are lonely for your daughter, Mrs Long?' she said, turning to speak to her over her shoulder. Mama had her long, fair hair in a plait today and it made her look so young. And pretty.

'Call me Nicola, please. And yes, I miss Sophie. Every hour of the day. But she's a complicated little girl, and I've probably been a little too soft with her. I don't approve of my ex taking her away,' she added quickly, 'but I do know that Ben won't take any nonsense from her. The only problem is, that some of the things that Ben might teach her might be a little … ill-judged. He can be a little too aspirational as far as Sophie's concerned.'

'He wants Sophie to be a doctor or something like that, doesn't he? Instead of an artist,' I ventured, grabbing one of Mama's homemade biscuits.

Nicola reached out for the steaming mug of coffee, then heaped two spoonfuls of sugar into it which surprised me. She sipped at her coffee, her hands wrapped tightly around the mug, her mouth opening and closing as if she was trying to find the right words.

'Yes, Magda, but it's not just that. He moves her from school to school, thinking that none of them are good enough for her. And he criticises the friend choices she makes.' She looked down into her coffee.

'You mean – friends like me?'

Nicola nodded and I could see Mama's eyes hardening. I knew she had followed most of the conversation so far. Tata sat silently on the sofa. Listening.

'Yes, Magda,' Nicola said, looking up now. 'Ben had a perfect little posh Chester Roader in mind as a friend for Sophie. Preferably from a rich background with parents in Law or Medicine,' she went on, shaking her head. 'And your grades were so much better than hers – he didn't like that.'

'Then, why did she become my friend?' I asked.

Nicola looked at me with kindness. 'To rebel, I suppose. To annoy her dad. Who knows? But when I met you for the first time, Magda, I knew you would be good for her. Rooted, honest, clever – you were all the things I wanted her to be.' She placed her hand on mine. 'I'm so sorry, Mr and Mrs Jankowski, but I wanted to be completely honest with you.' She looked up at my parents now, her eyes glazed again. 'And what she did with Toni – that was to get our attention too. To make us angry.

'And she did not think about the hurting to my family?' Mama asked, her voice breaking with anger.

'I don't think she was *thinking* at all, Mrs Jankowska. Just reacting. She thought I was choosing Charlie over her and she was fuming with her dad for flying in and bossing her around – as *she* saw it.'

'Are you going to telephone your ex-husband?' Tata asked evenly. 'I would like you to tell him everything that's happened and bring the child back to Belfast. I want my son's name cleared.' It was an order, not a request.

'Yes, Mr Jankowski,' she nodded, setting her mug down. 'That's exactly what I will do. And he *will* listen to me this time, because he won't want her associated with any 'untoward' incident that might blemish the image he's helped to create for her.'

'We would be most thankful for that,' Mama said. 'And call us Katarina and Tomasz,' she added. She smiled, but there was steel in her smile now. I could tell that she liked Sophie's mum, but she was no longer prepared to let anyone damage her family.

'And Sophie is welcome to come back here again. But only if she apologises first. To my son *and* my daughter,' Mama added.

Nicola nodded, pulling a tissue out of her pocket and wiping her eyes.

'Thank you. All of you,' she said, glancing at all three of us. 'You have been more than gracious about all of this. Oh, and Magda,' she said, taking my hand again. 'I truly believe that Sophie did see you as her friend. I *know* she admired you, but I know that she wronged you too. Maybe ... maybe when she comes back, you'll give her another chance?'

She was actually pleading with me – I could see it in her eyes. Neat, shiny Nicola with her Chester mansion and trendy art gallery. Nicola who had started life on the same streets as Colin but who had found a way out.

'Alright,' I said. 'But this time she has to be honest from the start. About everything.'

Chapter twenty-three

St Patrick's Day was one of the biggest and best days in Belfast in the spring. Colin said he went into the city centre every year for the parades, and this year he was taking me too. And Sophie.

'I seriously do not suit green hair!' Sophie was moaning.

'Then why did you dye it?' I asked, raising an eyebrow at her green-striped hair.

'I was trying to get into the *spirit* of things, Magda,' she grinned.

Of course, this was all part of the new Sophie Long. Getting down with the *common people*. Ever since she'd come back to Northern Ireland she'd insisted on getting to know the streets her mum had come from. She'd even met cousins she'd never seen before living a stone's throw from our flat. And speaking of stones – there had been no more of those. Colin may have been monosyllabic most of the time, but he'd obviously talked to someone who had talked to someone. It was all a bit vague, but I was more than grateful for it.

'You didn't try very hard, Magda,' Sophie said, elbowing me. 'Seriously – a green scarf? That's it?'

'I'm Polish, not Irish, Sophie. Remember? *Duh!*' I answered, elbowing her back.

'*Duh* – you can be whatever you want to be, Miss Jankowska! Remember the discussion we had in Citizenship class? *Self-knowledge* is what it's all about, not nationality.'

Self-knowledge was now Sophie's mantra. Since she'd come back from Thailand, she'd been going to Relate sessions with her mum to sort out her 'issues', and she'd become like a bloody preacher. Right enough though, a lot of it made sense. After the first few weeks of crying her eyes out, she'd come round to the idea that she *was* responsible for her own actions, but her mum and dad had also agreed to stop 'screwing her up' with their opposing ideas about how she should be raised. Her dad had decided to stop pestering her about her future and let her enjoy the present. Her mum was now working at the gallery three and a half days a week and spending more time with her. But it was our Toni who had really given her what for. That first time she came round to our flat, he had really laid it on the line with her.

It was a late January Saturday morning when she'd knocked on the door. Her face had been blotchy with tear-stains and she had dark shadows under her eyes. She had received a pretty cool reception from Mama and Tata that morning. She did all the apology stuff and the crying stuff and then Toni had asked her if she even knew what she was sorry for. I was so proud of my big brother that day.

'You have tried to manipulate everyone around you, Sophie,' he had said. 'And all you are ever concerned about is you – not how your actions affect other people. I could have lost my job – and worse – my good name. Did you even think about that?' His eyes had been flashing, angry.

'I … I am so sorry, Toni,' she'd said, tears dripping off her face. 'I never actually showed the photo to anyone. It was a lie that I had shared it with Paul. I – I wouldn't have done that to you.'

'Then why take it in the first place?' he asked, his voice even now but with controlled anger.

'To hurt my parents. To make them think that

they needed to spend more time with me. *Both* of them. Together.'

She could hardly get the words out now, she was sobbing so much. She was pitiful, sitting there like a little girl, outlining her plan to get her parents back together.

'But I know I was being stupid. And horrible!' she coughed out. Her nose was running now too and Mama passed her a tissue.

'I told Mrs Walsh everything, Toni. You won't lose your job,' she said, shaking her head before blowing her nose.

'Damn right I won't!' Toni shouted, making even Tata look at him wide-eyed. 'I have come to this country to make a life and I won't have a selfish, vain little girl like you mess it up for me!' He spoke through clenched teeth, barbed-wire tips on every word.

'Toni – that is now enough,' Mama warned him in English. 'Sophie knows she was wrong – there is no need to call her these names.'

Toni nodded, but said that she needed to change her ways or she would not be welcome around our family again.

She had literally begged for forgiveness then, and this time I think I believed her. She had spent the next few weeks baring her soul and promising me that there would be no more *frenemy* stuff.

'I never got why you were so well in with Mia and her Miseries one minute, and then been a cling-on with me the next,' I said to her.

'I wanted to keep you both on side, I guess. Dad always told me to keep your friends close and your enemies closer,' she said, unable to look me in the eye.

'Your dad sure gives such 'good' advice,' I sighed. 'The thing is, Sophie, which one was your enemy – me or Mia?'

'Both of you – in a way,' she admitted, her face reddening. 'You were the enemy because you're so clever and so – *sorted*. But Mia and her gang have teeth, so I was pathetic enough to keep them on side too.'

'Sorted? Me?'

'Yeah, you know your own mind. You do your own thing. I admired that. I still do.'

I was still a little wary, even now nearly two months later, but she had been true to her word. There was no more high drama, or fawning over me one minute and crying about me the next. She no longer had a phone so there were no more photos taken. In fact, she seemed to settle into herself – more calm and comfortable than I'd ever seen.

Toni, though, had kept her at arms' length ever

since and I had a feeling that he might never truly forgive her. He had confided in me that he had been frightened of losing Modesta's friendship over the whole thing. Thankfully that hadn't happened, and he had spent more and more evenings with her lately, their relationship blossoming into something that made Mama smile every time she saw them together.

Toni was kept busy at work though – he had taken over some of Tata's duties now that he was teaching part-time in Belview. Mrs Walsh had asked him to take a Horticulture class with the Year 11s, with a view to entering them for their GCSE in it the following year. To say it was right up his street was an understatement: teaching *and* planting at the same time! Mama was still grieving for Dziadek – as we all were – but was going beyond the shop and flat a little more these days, and picking up more English along the way. In fact, she was going to join Sophie, Colin and me later beside the City Hall and watch the parades with us. We were hoping to meet Anna there too. Tata was busy at home marking coursework for his new Horticulture class.

By 11.30 the Belfast streets were thronged. Floats of every shape and size were lined up along Royal Avenue, with a giant effigy of a grey-bearded St Patrick on the first one. The streets had been rinsed clean by rain the night before, but for now the sky was a perfect pale blue. Irish dancers entertained us in front of the City Hall and, for a change, the sun shone and the city smiled.

Sophie and I were trying out a few of our own Irish dance moves, embarrassing the hell out of Colin, when Anna arrived. She looked at us under her fringe, staring at us as if we had finally lost the plot – and for some reason that made us laugh until our stomachs hurt. Colin shook his head at Anna and she almost-smiled back, and weirdly I felt a bit jealous.

Then the floats were on the move and the parade started at 12 noon on the dot, snaking its away along Chichester Street, towards Custom House Square and onwards in the direction of the River Lagan. Shamrock banners shook in the air alongside green balloons and plastic snakes. Kilted pipers marched past us and people in costumes of every description: everything from Daleks to men with top hats walking on stilts. A Delorean sports car even floated past, followed by half of a *Titanic* model.

Mama was linking my arm by now as we followed the crazy crowd, who were speaking in every language under the sun. You didn't have to be just Irish or British to live in Belfast – I could see that now. And hear it.

'You enjoying yourself, Mama?' I asked.

'Very much, Magda,' she answered, squeezing my arm. She tried to speak in English most of the time now when she was out and about, but of course at home we spoke Polish.

We let ourselves be carried along by the wave of walkers, laughing and soaking up the atmosphere of *Béal Feirste*, my adopted city – its name means something like 'rivermouth of the sandbar'. Sophie was pointing at Irish dancers in curly wigs and elaborate dresses and laughing about the time her dad had made her join a dancing class.

'I just couldn't get the hang of all those high leg-flips,' she giggled. 'And the bloody school hall we practised in was always *freezing*! It was more like *Shiverdance* than *Riverdance*. Dad was so cross with me when I gave it up.'

At least she was laughing about it – and calling him Dad now instead of Ben. For a month or so after she'd come back from Thailand she couldn't mention him without getting upset. Now, though, she seemed to accept that she wouldn't be the person he wanted her to be – she would be herself instead. And from the sound of the Skype calls she'd been having with him, he'd come to accept that as well. It was kind of weird that her parents had over-expectations of Sophie and Mama had seemed to have under-expectations of me. Or so I thought. But the letter from Dziadek had changed all that.

Mama had let me read the letter about a week after we had come back from Poland as she cuddled into bed beside me on a cold Saturday morning. She said that she had wanted to give me time to absorb everything that had happened before I read it.

'You were not in good place, Magda – what with the Sophie business, losing Dziadek and coming back from Poland. I know you are still unhappy about these things, but maybe my papa's words will help you now. Read it, my love.'

She slipped me the sheet of paper and I trembled as I began to read. It was written in Polish of course but here it is in English:

Dear Magda,

When you read this I will be gone – but, I hope, not forgotten. I will be with my other Magda and I will be at peace. But I know this will be hard for you, my little one. I have worried so much about you since we came to live in this city.

I have known about your battles here, Magda, every single day – the stones, the name-calling and the Belview Beetches (I believe that is what you sometime called them.) But, you know, this little

*country has so much to give to you in good things
too.*

I looked up at Mama and she nodded. She knew
these things too. 'Read on,' she said, kissing my
forehead.

*You may think I was wasting away in my room,
sitting by the window. But I was actually watching
and learning about this new home. My heart was
heavy always, remembering Gizycko, but then I
saw hills change from spring to summer to autumn
to winter: snow-capped one month and full with
blossom the next. And I saw the Mourne
Mountains and the Irish Sea when Toni drove us to
Newcastle. Huge grey-blue water – bigger than the
lakes at home – with white tips on the grey waves.
And curlews and gannets and oystercatchers, all
wheeling and dancing in the big sky. And little
villages and harbours along the way with stacked
nets and fishing fleets.*

*And there are friends too, Magda. They can come
in all shapes and sizes – damaged, broken, but not
beyond repair. Give Sophie a chance and Anna and
Colin. Yes, I see Colin watching our home, envying
us. He is not a skinny, scared boy any more and he
has you to thank for that.*

Look after your mama and Tata and Toni too. I hope he will marry Modesta someday and be as happy as I was. And I hope you will go to the Queen's University you showed me. Walk those hallowed halls with pride, Magda. Hold your head up and know that you are brave and strong and clever. Because you are. You will be professor someday, or doctor or lawyer. But whatever you become, you must be you. <u>Always</u> be you.

My heart and soul are heavy now, my granddaughter, but you must be light and flowing. And sparkling – like this sapphire stone I enclose for you. Your birthstone. Because stones aren't always for hurting, Magda. This one is for love.

Dziadek

XXX

I realised I was biting the inside of my cheek. The taste of blood made me want to cry like a baby. Instead breath had curled in hard puffs from my nostrils.

'Here it is, Magda. He had this made for you last autumn. Isn't it beautiful?' Mama was lifting a silver chain out of a box with a sparkling sapphire pendant attached. 'He wanted you to have this when the time was right. *When you were ready to look at the sky again and see the future.* His words, my love.'

231

And that morning, with Mama's face tipped towards mine, our noses just touching, I knew I would make a life for myself here. I didn't know if I would live as long as Dziadek, or whether I would stay in Ireland forever, but I knew what mattered. I would make the most of the time I would be given. I would climb up to Cavehill with Colin and we would look down on this beautiful city emerging from its past, at Belfast Lough with its mudflats and rocky shores and all the sculptures and landmarks that marked a city at peace.

And Sophie Long? Maybe she would be with us and maybe she wouldn't. She had confessed that the sketch she had done of Toni all those months ago *had* been a bit of a piss-take – but it had also been a genuine present. Maybe Sophie would never be straight with me – maybe she was never destined to walk the *line of truth*.

But one thing was for sure, Magda Jankowska would no longer walk in shadows.

The End

Now that you're hooked why not try
Knock Back
also published by Poolbeg

Here's a sneak preview of chapter one.

Chapter one

So, there we were, driving along these narrow, country roads to Knockmore Farm – this special place in the countryside that treats kids like me. I had read that it was a place that helped *'families in crisis'*, but my family wasn't in crisis. Apparently, it was just me that was the problem. And, of course, good old Mum and Dad looked on the bright side and said it was all for the best.

'You'll love it, Ben – living and working on a farm for the summer. Taking care of horses, chickens, cows ...You'll get a new perspective, love.'

Whatever that meant! All I could imagine was chicken-shit and cattle-muck, but if that's where they wanted to send me, then bring it on! After all, it was my idea in the first place. Dad hadn't actually found that page in the *Belfast Telegraph* by himself. I'd put it there on the coffee table right in front of the TV, exactly on the spot where he'd put his feet up and watch Man City. **'Knockmore Farm – A Residential Centre for Helping Teenagers Build Self-esteem.'** Mum's social-worker mate had told me about it. But I wasn't interested in building anything. All I wanted to do was to find out the truth and if it meant looking at bovine mammals for twelve hours a day, then so be it!

I did my best to look peeved about it and locked

myself in my room for a few hours. I felt bad about upsetting Amy, though. She was only seven and still thought I was God's gift. I really hadn't *meant* to trample her corn snake, but when she saw the squishy remains of Sindy the Snake she nearly screamed the house down, and she was even worse when she heard I was going to be sent away over it.

'*He didn't mean it, Mum! It was an accident!*' she had shrieked down the stairs.

Her wee hands were covered in snake-guts and I just knew she would have tried to hide the whole mess if it wasn't for Mum finding her hovering over Sindy's corpse.

'For God's sake, Ben! *What* were you thinking of?' Mum rolled her eyes to the high heavens for maybe the tenth time that day. '*Why* did you take her out of her tank in the first place? And then prance about and end up trampling her?'

What could I say? That I was Saint Patrick the Second? Nah, I just shook my head and retreated, letting Mum and Dad jump to conclusions and decide on my fate. They must have stayed up until after midnight talking in, like, *really* loud whispers. I could hear Dad complain about my deteriorating behaviour and Mum saying it was just 'a call for attention'.

Amy cheered up a bit though when I told her that Sindy had gone to Snake Heaven: a sort of paradise of coiled snakes slithering away to their scales' content. She loved the idea that they might drop down from there: millions of snakes falling from the sky while people did their shopping – or sat on the bog – or whatever. She has a BIG imagination, my wee sister!

I spent the evening before my departure trying to pack for my Bear Grylls experience at Knockmore. Trouble was, I hadn't a clue what I'd need. I didn't even *own* a pair of wellies – well, you don't have much need for rubber boots in the suburbs. I packed a few T-shirts and jeans and stuff and then spent about half an hour wondering whether I'd need a torch or matches or, you know, survival kind of gear. I could be sleeping under the stars for all I knew! I took a look at my clean, comfy bed in my not-so-clean, comfy room and wondered when I'd next have a decent night's sleep. Our house was on a tree-lined avenue – no bellowing bulls or crowing cockerels to wake you at an unearthly hour. No tractors thrumming past your window when you're trying to sleep through your alarm. The noisiest thing on Chester Road was probably my mum's dolphin music!

'Ben? Can I come in?'

It was Mum's Guilty Voice – the one she uses when she thinks she's failed as a parent. Without waiting for an answer, she came in and sat down on the edge of my bed. She started picking through my holdall and I noticed the lines on her forehead crease up when she saw the box of matches.

'Well, there mightn't be any electricity. How am I supposed to know what I need?' I grumbled. Then I realised she thought I had a more sinister use for them in mind. Well, there *was* my chip-pan experiment in the back garden that had gone slightly wrong ... 'Crikey, Mum, what do you think I am? A flippin' arsonist?'

'Please don't swear, Ben. You know I don't think that. I just ... I just wasn't sure why you were taking them. Listen, there's every convenience at Knockmore, *including* electric lights, so I can safely say you can leave the matches at home. Now, how are you feeling about all this? About Knockmore?'

'How do you think I'm feeling?' I answered, without looking at her. 'I'm thinking you and Dad reckon I'm a delinquent and you can't wait to see the back of me for two months.'

I could hear the sigh, the long, slow release of breath that said I was being unreasonable – *again* – and that they were at their wits' end about me – *again!* But I wasn't going to make it easy on them, even if I did have my own agenda at the funny farm. Part of me felt guilty for hurting her like this. Part of me hated her for twelve years of lies.

She stopped speaking after that and left me to it.

She didn't say a word to me this morning either, and the journey to Knockmore felt like a funeral. Nobody, I mean *nobody* spoke.

Belfast streets gave way to these windy roads that should have been off-road tracks, and the way Dad was driving I thought I was going to have to get out and *push* the car! Mum kept looking round at me with these big sad eyes but Dad didn't flinch. He stared straight at that road ahead because there was just *no way* he was going to take a wrong turn – he was taking me to Knockmore by hook or by crook, even if it took all day to get there. Apparently he'd had enough of my smart-ass personality of late and seriously believed that Knockmore was going to bring his son back. Whatever!

Then we came over a hill and I saw Strangford Lough loom up below us like a big puddle, with little islands splattered through the middle of it. And it was actually quite cool. I thought I could see these grey seals bobbing on the shoreline and part of me started to feel good about this whole thing. But then I looked at Amy – her chin was doubled on her chest and her lips were pouting like a goldfish – and I started to have second thoughts. All I had to do was say sorry and promise to make an effort and I knew Mum would have Dad turn the car round faster than a Ferrari. Well, a Ford Focus in our case. But I wouldn't do that. There was way too much at stake.

Down the hill we went and then started to climb steadily again. Then, following a sign, we turned in through a big pillared gate and up a long driveway, still climbing gradually, until we came to a stop in front of a big country-house type building, with a modern, glass-panelled, glitzy bit attached.

I could feel the sea breathing on me as soon as I opened the car door. A plane, probably an Easyjet fifty-five hours behind schedule, drew a thin white line across the sky. Mum was watching the lough swelling below and I just knew she was going to go all bloody philosophical on me. Well, at least she was speaking to me again.

'You know, this is a time to grow, Ben.' She breathed out. 'And a time to reap what you sow.'

Seriously – I could *not* handle another farming metaphor! She'd been coming out with them for over a week now – apparently my stay here would 'bear fruit' and allow my 'fertile imagination' time to mature. After a while I couldn't even hear them – they'd become like white noise – but now they were getting to me again.

'Look at this place! It's paradise, Ben. You'll be a man when you leave here!'

Technically, no – I would still be a teenager, but I let that one pass. She'd been in a funny mood ever since I was signed up for this place, convincing herself that it was the right thing to do. Poor Mum – she was always looking for 'solutions' – but hey, sometimes you just couldn't fix things. She pushed her hand through her hair and sighed like it was going to be her last breath.

Me, I was still focusing on the waves below us and thinking about throwing off my trainers and letting the water cut into my skin. But I was no Water Baby – that was Amy. She was the one who would love splashing about in the lough, feeling the white tips of spray against her shins. But Amy just stood there, with her hair all over her face, the colour of a blackbird.

Dad, though, he was already hauling my suitcase out of the car and striding across to the '*Knockmore Farm Reception*' in the glitzy part.

Right enough, the place didn't look like a lunatic asylum – more like one of those country spa houses Mum went to when she needed 'Me Time' – part olde worlde, part modern chic. But I wasn't going to be taken in that easily. They probably had sweatshops out the back and torture chambers for snake-squishers.

'*Therapeutic Learning Environment*', it said across the top of the reception desk. A woman with short bobbed hair and a name badge that said *Kate Bridges* was beaming at us from behind the desk. She made a brief welcome speech and Dad signed a few papers. Then Kate Bridges confiscated my mobile phone, smarmily explaining that no phones were allowed 'for the duration'. *Crap*. I hadn't expected that.

Dad looked around the place, nodding his head as if he had found Nirvana. He scanned all the phrases that zig-zagged around the walls: *Positive Behaviour, Mutual Respect, Self-discipline*. Then he looked at me like he was going to deliver a Dad Lecture, his eyes all piercing and serious, so I asked Kate where the nearest bog was and took off upstairs.

I could see fields that went on forever through a large window at the top of the stairs and there were three or four horses down below me in one of them. I stood there, watching their mouths munching on grass as if they didn't have a care in the world, breath steaming from them. Then I noticed some two-storey modern buildings that looked like classrooms at the back of the main building. Great! So *that's* where the punishment would begin!

When I went back downstairs Dad and Kate Bridges were gone. I had a nosy round. There was a large kitchen to the back of reception, which I thought an odd place to have one. Probably the kitchen in the main house was too old-fashioned – in the basement maybe, like a lot of them were in the old days. A few people were busying themselves cooking but they didn't see me taking a sneak peek.

'Ben? Are you there? Come on, son – Mr Wilson's waiting to talk to us.'

Dad again. All grave and commanding.

Wilson was the owner of Knockmore House and director of the 'troubled teens' programme – which was funded by all sorts of benefactors and grants of course.

I followed Dad along the hallway that joined the glitzy part to the main house and then to a big room with a huge, dark, round wooden table in the centre.

Mr Wilson (in a suit), Kate Bridges and another woman were sitting there, smiling at me as if my lights were on but there was nobody in. Amy and Mum were already beside them.

'Hello, Ben.' Wilson waved a hand, indicating that we should sit down.

We sat.

'I'm John Wilson. This is Allie Cooper our farm manager – you've already met Kate Bridges our admissions officer.'

Kate and John the Head Honcho still had smiles pasted on their faces – but it was Allie Cooper who seemed to really focus on me and take me in. I felt her eyes puncture mine like she was searching for something, so I searched right back. Her eyes were a kind of hazel – goldy-green – but I looked so hard I could see these little brown speckles in them. Like a song thrush. Weird!

'Ben, would you like to tell us why you're here?' asked the Head Honcho, twitching his monobrow which crawled across his forehead like a caterpillar.

'Because I squished a snake?'

'Well, it wasn't just that, Ben. There were, em, *other* incidents too, weren't there?' he said, still smiling.

'Ye...es,' I answered. Bloody hell, did he want me to list them?

Dad shook his head as if he wished the ground would swallow him up.

'But we're not interested in going through a litany of your offences today, Ben – we're interested in talking about how we can change things.' The Honcho shook his head repeatedly.

I was afraid if he kept doing it his comb-over would flop back over. And I did *not* want to see that.

I was relieved that we didn't have to go through my *litany of offences* because I couldn't remember half of them anyway. Crashing into a hearse on my bike, peeing into the Guides' campfire, that chippan experiment – I could remember those at least. The thing is, I wasn't a *bad* lad, just a lad who screwed up a lot – but I had to screw up, because it was the only way to get to Knockmore.

After nearly half an hour of pep talk, the Honcho walked Mum and Dad out. Me and Amy followed.

Mum looked like she'd changed her mind about the whole thing but Dad was sticking to his guns.

'He has to do it, Claire. He has to find himself.'

Huh – now *that* was ironic! *Find* myself?

I rolled my eyes and let them say their goodbyes: Mum all weepy and perfumey and Dad straight as a single 4-iron. Then I squeezed Amy's hand and made her promise not to hate me.

'I'll buy you new snakes, Ames, I promise. Big fat scary ones – just the way you like them, okay?'

'Poisonous?' she asked hopefully, her blue eyes peeking at me from under her flap of a fringe.

'Maybe not, Ames, just to be on the safe side. Come and see me, though. Okay?'

''Kay.'

The car drove off. Amy waved from the back seat and I thought I saw Mum dabbing at her eyes in the mirror. Dad looked straight ahead. I stood there and watched the car crinkling the air and shining on the long driveway of Knockmore.

Two months. I had just two months to find out everything I needed to know. Either I was completely freakin' bonkers for coming here or I was on the cusp of the biggest discovery of my life. There was only one way to find out and I had the strangest feeling something or someone was waiting for me, right here at Knockmore.